AUGUST SPIVEY, P.I.

by
Mike Keenan

This book is based on true events, but it is a work of fiction. Names, characters, places, incidents and timelines may have been changed for dramatic purposes. Certain characters may be composites, or entirely fictitious."

Printed in the United States
Published: First Look Publishing (Austin)
Version 1.0

Print ISBN: 978-1-7326642-2-7
Digital ISBN: 978-1-7326642-3-4

Cover Graphics: Brian Burrowes
Editing: Stetham Communication, LLC
Printed by Kindle Direct Publishing

STORIES

I dedicate this book to my brother, Pat, a real-life August Spivey.

1

WHAT HAPPENED AT THE RIO

I agreed to serve Neal Green's civil paper even-though I knew better. You see, Neal and I didn't get along. But, he needed me and I needed the business, so he and I met in his law office and had a talk about how I'd serve Tommy Grubbs.

Next morning, I was up early. The alarm clock never had a chance. I chased a sweet-roll with a couple of gulps of black coffee and then hit the road for Book, Texas, a two-hour drive. I owned a used 1977 Ford pickup. Bought it in 1992 at an auction for $600. It had fifteen years and 100,000 miles on it at the time. I think it was red once. When I drove her, she was a rusty old bucket. Died on me at 250,000 miles. I loved that truck. It was loyal as a dog.

The route I chose had plenty of treeless open country. Even now I don't like big trees. You put a bunch of big trees together, it could result in a forest. I go anywhere *near* the woods and I get a case of the claustrophobic. You never know what's coming at you out of the trees.

I've been to Book, Texas several times. People there are like people everywhere. They're born, they die, in between they've got their problems. It's me who tells them when those problems need a lawyer. I rolled into Book that day with my stomach growling. I stopped and stepped into a convenience store for a bottle of iced tea and a packaged sandwich.

"I'm looking for this man," I said.

"Haven't seen him," said the guy behind the counter. He was big and polite. He gave me back the picture I handed him.

"You got an address?" he asked. "Maybe I can point you the right way."

I drove into a tough-looking neighborhood not far from the store. It was 1:00, hotter than hell. I was taking a nice little sauna in the cab of my truck.

I pulled into the parking lot of a small apartment complex that had the shape of a rectangle. Alley on the backside, blue dumpster wedged into a corner, the place held twelve units, six in front, six in back, all of them opening directly to the outside.

I found the name *Tommy Grubbs* on a battery of mailboxes near a staircase on the side of the complex. I walked around to the alley and stopped at Grubbs's apartment. I knocked. A young woman, maybe twenty, answered the door. A pair of cut-off jeans hugged on her pretty good. The best and worst of her was up top. God love her, she had horrible teeth. Made me want to look the other way. Get past the teeth, a guy could fall into her at night.

I peeked in the apartment, a one-room efficiency with a bed, a table, and a couch. Off to the right was a kitchenette I doubt two adults could fit in. A box fan filled a window.

"Tommy ain't here. He's drivin' today. All I got to say."

"He's gonna get served, one way or another," I said.

On her hip was a baby, not old enough to walk. Behind her, in the glow of a TV, sat a girl.

"Mimi, come here," said the woman.

The girl jumped up, walked to the door where she stood at the woman's side. She was an angel. Big brown eyes, skin like fresh cream, give her time, she'd be wrapping guys around her little finger.

"Mimi, who's your daddy?"

"My daddy is Tommy Grubbs," said the girl.

"Do you love your daddy?"

"Yes."

"Why, honey?"

"My daddy loves me. He serves Our Lord, Jesus Christ."

"Who's your mommy?"

"You are."

"Who's your real mommy?"

"Mona Grubbs."

"Is your real mommy a nice lady?"

"No."

"You want to live with her?"

"No."

"How come, sweetie?"

"She's a sinner."

"You can go watch TV now, Mimi."

The woman waited until the little girl sat down.

"You see what you're up against?" she asked.

Long as I've been at this, I still get a kick out of people thinking it's me suing them. I got it across to her I was only the messenger. She witnessed me that they were Christians, willing to give Caesar what was Caesar's. Tommy Grubbs would be there in the morning, only I better show up early because he was a working-man who hit the ground running.

I went back to the convenience store where I used the pay phone to call my wife, Sandy. I've known Sandy a long time. We met when I was bartending and she was waitressing. A lot of guys hit on her, but I got lucky. She puts up with my bullshit, and that's not easy. Sandy was an army brat. Her dad was in the military. They lived all over. She spent her childhood years in Germany. German is a second language to her. Whenever I piss her off, she curses me in a way that would make an interpreter blush.

Before cell phones, I kept a roll of quarters in the ashtray of my truck. It made no sense me driving one hundred miles back home then doing it again the next day. Best thing for me was a motel, then serve Tommy Grubbs in the morning. Sandy agreed.

I asked the guy in the convenience store where I might get a motel nearby with a pool. He gave me two, the *Rio* and the *Orion*. Both, he was sure, had pools.

The *Rio* looked to have the cleaner pool so I went with it. I've always enjoyed laying in the sun. It feels good, helps me unwind. I figured to sun, shower, grab a meal, then hit the hay.

I checked in using my credit card. It was as plastic and pretty as the one Bill Gates probably carries now, but I'm sure that's where it ends. I told the Chinaman working the desk I wanted a room with an air conditioner that blew plenty of cold air. The *Rio* was your typical small-town motel. Nothing fancy, it looked clean on the outside. A chain-link fence kept kids away from the pool. It grabbed my attention there were no cars in the lot. Middle of a weekday in a small town, I let it go.

I walked through a pink door into a dark room. Dark enough that I could barely see. A thick curtain over the window blocked out most of the light.

I set down the overnight bag I kept in my trunk, and then felt for the lamp on a dresser off to my right. Directly in front of me was a wall that had a spot on it. A big black thing. Took up most of the wall. Reminded me of a stain. I swore I saw the thing move, but in the dark, first thing that came to me was that the wall was damp.

I looked left, and then right. Those walls were moving too. When I say moving, I mean this big stain that covered everything was sort of shifting right there before my eyes, and changing shape, throbbing, and behaving like no wet spot I'd seen in my life so far.

I had one place left to look and that was the ceiling. It had the stain too. The whole room was one, big, connected, slithering stain.

I punched a small button at the bottom of the lamp waiting for my eyes to get right. Back of my neck, I felt something. It went through my mind the label on my shirt needed clipping. A couple of more things hit me on my bare arms. I wondered what was going on. All over I got hit; face, hair, with something that made me feel like I was outside standing in the rain. "Mother of God!" I yelled and then ran like hell out of the room.

Let's get clear about something. I've got nothing against the Chinese. The yellow man has his American story same as the rest of us. His people came over on a boat, built the railroads, held on tight with all ten fingers to keep what they earned. My people came over on a boat too. Probably worked the same railroad. Everybody's got a right to taste the American pie.

"No leefund," said the Chinaman. A sign on the wall behind him said as much.

"Bullshit," I said. I almost laughed. I *guarangoddamnteed* him I would get my money back.

I told him how I walked into the room. How the whole place was lousy with roaches. The big ones, the B-52s of the insect world. On the ceiling, on the walls. I told him how I switched on the light and they swarmed me thinking I was food, or a tree, or the queen-mamma from where they came. I told him how I ran out of the room, stripped off my clothes, down to my bare butt, thinking an army of bugs was crawling up my ass.

"No leefund," he said.

The Chinaman's wife and a small kid were holed up in a dinky room the other side of the desk. The kid was screaming blue heebie-jeebies loud enough it made me wonder how the hell the Chinaman kept his marbles.

He said something to his wife in *Charley Chan* and then he and I took a walk. At the door to my room I saw the light was off. In the crazy blur of roaches coming at me, I must've hit its switch.

"Make sure you turn the light on," I suggested.

I let him go in first. When the light went on, I backed out of the room and shut the door. I pulled hard on the knob. The Chinaman was going to get every bit of what I got from that room.

"I car porice," he yelled. "Ret me out! I no rie. I car porice!"

"I call Health Department," I yelled back.

He and I played tug-o-war on the door knob. He pulled hard. I held tight to my end.

"I give leefund. I give leefund."

"Promise?" I asked.

"I plomise," he yelled.

I let loose of the door. He came running out like a guy who'd just been swarmed by a million filthy roaches. He was jabbering all sorts of *gobbledeegook*, pulling his hair and in no shape to talk. I gave him a minute to settle down.

"Pull it in. You can still come out of this a man," I said.

I felt sort of sorry for him. I had to figure his ball and chain made for a pretty lousy frame of mind. How did bastards like him get out of bed in the morning? The same went for Tommy Grubbs. For some guys, the losing started when the alarm went off.

Back in the office, we did business. With my money back, I thought seriously about driving home then coming back in the morning. If I wanted to serve Grubbs, that was out of the question. I stopped in at the *Orion* feeling like I'd swallowed a lit firecracker.

A quick look-see into the mind of August Spivey might explain a little. Put me in a room with a pit-bull, if he doesn't eat me, I'm OK in about an hour. Put me in a room with a cockroach, any cockroach, especially if he's on the wall, I'm fucked-up for a week.

The guy who designed the *Rio* must've designed the *Orion* too. If motels were people, the *Rio* and the *Orion* would be twins; same layout, same office, same dinky apartment behind the desk.

A leathery old girl named Grace Smalley ran the *Orion*. Grace had bible-belt written all over her. She was hanging up the phone when I walked in.

"Must be nice thinking the whole world is pulling for you," she said.

"Do you mean me?" I asked.

"No, I meant my granddaughter. That girl has slept with every bad man in Book. She's tried every drug imaginable. Pregnant? Of course. Job? Fired too many times to count. And then she runs home to my daughter and my son-in-law and they love her to death. That was my daughter on the phone whining about 'Cindy this' and 'Cindy that.' They spoiled the girl rotten. Now they're paying for it. The world should be kind to its children but it shouldn't be run by them. Oh my! I don't even know you!"

7

"I want a room," I said.

From the get-go, Grace Smalley and I got along like peanut butter and jelly. I told her about what happened at the *Rio*.

"We got no roaches here. Nothing like you described. Well, we got a few. This is Texas, God sakes."

She insisted we do a walk through the room I'd be renting. The room was dark, with an air conditioner blasting out cold air, a clone of the room I had at the *Rio*. Grace pulled the curtain back flooding the room with light.

"Looks better when you can see, don't it?"

"Over at the *Rio* all the walls and the ceiling were crawling with roaches. Room just like this so lousy with roaches you couldn't see the plaster on the walls," I said.

"Darlin," said Grace, "you see one roach in this room tonight, I'll give your money back."

I sat out by the pool sipping a *Budweiser* I bought from my favorite convenience store. Beer and sun calmed me down. I found a Mexican diner that looked clean where I bought a carry-out of chicken enchiladas, brown rice, and black beans. I had the waiter pile on the picante sauce. I love my Mexican food nose-running hot. I ate it back at the motel watching a re-run of *Moonlighting* with Bruce Willis and Cybil Shepherd. (I like private eye T.V. Go figure.) Then, I showered and fell into bed.

I'm like the next guy when it comes to sleep. I don't sleep good, the next day I have a hole in my head. I sleep good, it's like my brain had a square meal. I stared at the ceiling, thinking mostly about bugs.

When I was a kid, I had the solar system pasted on my bedroom ceiling. It glowed at night. I'd lay there looking at those fake stars, pretending I was camping. Whenever I can't sleep, I take myself back there.

Next morning, I stopped by the office to pay my bill. I let Grace know the *Orion* was my new headquarters in Book. She asked me how I slept. I was happy to tell her no roaches came a calling.

Later I knocked on Tommy Grubbs's apartment. He stepped outside wearing gym shorts and a T-shirt. That box fan was still pulling in air.

"So, what do I do with this?" he whispered.

"I'd read it," I said.

"Yeah, but then what?"

"You got a lawyer?"

His eyes darted from the door of his shabby apartment to a worn-out Plymouth Duster parked a few feet away.

"Oh yeah, the best money can buy."

I mentioned to him that there was a legal-aide clinic in this county, that likely someone from this little village of his had used the poor-man's lawyer a time or two. He might ask around. I also told him to move fast on that piece of paper he was holding since time is very important in a lawsuit.

As I drove home that afternoon I did some math. My flat rate for Neal was seventy-five bucks. Figure the room, the meals, the gas at sixty dollars, *Operation Book* netted me fifteen bucks. That's good money if you're a teen-age kid in the lawn-mow business.

That night, I took it easy. I threw a couple of steaks on the grill. I ate my beef vampire-rare. I loaded up a baked potato with sour cream, butter, and cheese. For desert, I covered up a wedge of hot apple pie with two heavy scoops of vanilla ice cream that will one day, I'm sure, help send me to the ER. Goddamn that was good! A man couldn't ask for a better meal.

Sandy and I capped off the evening with a history show on network TV. Somebody building a road near Berlin dug up a battlefield full of Romans and Germans caught up a couple of thousand years ago in the beauty of slaughter. Way I see it, people haven't changed much in a long time.

2

WHEN NICE DON'T WORK

Tommy Ferris, a lawyer out of Houston, hired me to serve paper on a fella by the name of Todd Sparks. The way Ferris put it, Sparks was an ex-college football player with a short fuse who got his way by bullying people. He was the defendant in a nasty divorce suit brought by his wife who got fed up with his appetite for younger women.

I found Sparks at a park near his car dealership playing tennis with a woman who looked the shy side of twenty-five. I understood where the angry wife came from. The girl was sweet. It wouldn't surprise me at all if one day she made her living wearing nothing in front of a camera. Sparks was in his forties.

I brought my buddy, Sylvester Steele, along with me. Sylvester was a trust baby. He never worked a day in his life. Living-it-up was his job.

Syl had a hard-on for action. I had him ride shotgun and run my hand-held camera just to cover my ass when I worried things might get rough. I never thought I'd get sweet on technology, but there you go.

I parked at the curb about one-hundred feet from the tennis courts. There were two courts, side by side, surrounded by a tall, chain-link fence. A young, black couple was playing on the court next to Sparks and his girlfriend.

"Todd Sparks," I said.

I was standing inside the fence, not far from the net that separated Sparks from his girl.

"Yeah," he said. "Who are you?"

I identified myself as August Spivey, ordered by court to deliver civil process on him. An easy shot, lobbed over by his girlfriend, came across the net. His return-shot went lousy, landing out of bounds. The next thing I knew, his racket was flying at the net.

Now, here's where you've got to love the laws in the great State of Texas when it comes to the delivery of civil process. Let's say a guy refuses service, he won't take it in his hands, maybe he's sitting around his pool grilling meat, you know its him, you come up on him and he laughs then tells you to go to Hell, you just have to put your paper within arm's reach of him.

I put my paper under the racket which sat a few feet away.

"Hey," he said. "Get away from my racket."

"You're served," I said.

"I'm talking to you," he said. "I'm not gonna tell you again. Pick up that racket and get that shit out from under it."

I shrugged. He was in pretty good shape, but at forty or more, had some visible blubber under his T-shirt. I turned to walk away when I saw him bull-rush me like a linebacker blindsiding a quarterback.

I faced him. I sure as hell wasn't going to run. Man or mouse? I went with the man-choice. He took a wild, roundhouse swing at my head. I ducked, feeling his fist graze the top of my cap. Down low, I got a good look at his belly but I couldn't see his eyes, a bad thing in a fight. You always want to read the other guy's eyes.

There was a lot of fat to work with between his ribs and his kidneys. I caught him sweet, in a roll of goo on his right side, with an uppercut that went all the way to Dallas.

"Hooooooooooooooooooo!" he grunted, and then squashed out a fart that sounded like a canon going off.

I stepped back to get my balance as he doubled over. Now it was him looking down at the ground, me watching things from up top. He threw a pair of wild punches, one with each hand, that drew nothing but air. I came from under with four left-right uppercuts, *pop, pop, pop, pop*, to his face that left my knuckles wet.

He raised up and I saw the damage. Red snot leaked from his nose. Up the side of his left cheek crawled a gray mouse. His eyes were soft, round.

"We can let this go," I offered.

"Fuck you," he huffed.

He came at me. I caught him with a punch that should've been on sports television; one he walked into directly. It started in my toes, rose up through my hips and back, the power traveling down my shoulder, arm, and knuckles. I pasted his mug just below the nose. He and a couple of adult teeth took the elevator down.

I stood over him while he tried to get up. His girlfriend had her hand over her mouth. Sylvester came running up from the car and, with no direction from me, got the names and phone numbers of the black couple who had joined the party.

Sparks got up on his hands and knees, wobbly as a new-born calf trying out its legs for the first time.

"Had enough?" I asked.

He raised his hand, waived it *no mas* style, then rolled over on his back.

"Cindy," he whispered. "You saw all this, right?"

"Be quiet, Todd. Just stay still and be quiet," she said.

I picked up the paper and tossed it on his chest.

"You're served," I said.

In the car, Sylvester was wired like he'd just swallowed down ten cups of very strong coffee.

"August, I got it all on tape. Man oh man! What the hell got into you?"

"Sometimes," I said, "nice don't work."

I pretended like it was no big thing, but I couldn't remember the last time I felt that good.

3

UP-CLOSE AND PERSONAL

I got a call from Jack, my lawyer brother. He asked me if would I help out a woman friend of his, a lady who worked with him once upon a time. She needed somebody good at following people. She was out of work and out of money. Jack said he'd pay me. But I couldn't take money from Jack, as good as he'd been to me, so I reached into the purest, pro-bono part of my heart and made a visit to Keri Bruce thinking someday Saint Peter might be impressed.

"He's a good boy," she said. "Troubled, yes. But bad, no. His father abandoned my sister and him before he could walk. My brother-in-law was a worthless louse if there ever was one. And my sister is so beaten down emotionally that she can't manage my nephew."

Bruce lived in a nice little house with a nice little yard in an old part of town that was about fifty-fifty renters and owners. By the look of things inside, germs weren't welcome. She and I sat at the kitchen table drinking coffee. Up close, she was closing in on fifty but she looked pretty good for a gal that age. She was trim and came across as all-business. From the impression I got, any guy who wanted south of the border would need a ring and a request that comes on one knee.

"Here," she said.

She handed me a picture of her nephew. The kid was nineteen. He looked like a young colt. A pair of dull eyes told me experience and hard knocks were most of the schooling he'd get.

"He's never had a real girlfriend until now. As you can see from his photo, he's a good-looking kid. But he can't relate to women his age. He's a nineteen-year-old man with a ten-year-old's maturity."

She handed me another picture, one of him and a young girl taken in a photo booth.

"She's fifteen, Mr. Spivey. You know what that means."

I looked at the picture. On close look, the girl was no more than fifteen like Bruce said. But she was well-developed and made up to look much older. She had big-girl parts that could land you in jail and a spot on the sexual-bad-guy list.

"Yeah," I said. "So, what's the problem?"

Bruce went on to tell me that the girl's parents laid down the law with their daughter. They didn't want Bruce's nephew coming near their kid.

"The Daly's got a peace-bond on Ronny. He can't come within two hundred feet of the family, the house, or the girl. I'm glad. That might be the only way to keep him out of trouble."

"You think it will work?" I asked.

"Until this morning I thought it might. But now I think it's blowing up."

"What happened?" I asked.

"Some of my sister's jewelry is missing. She has so little. He took that, we're sure. She said he acted funny this morning when he left for work. I think he and that girl are going to make a run."

"Have you called the family?"

"Yes, they kept her home today. They hadn't seen him as of mid-morning."

"Let's say I follow him over there. What then?"

"Call me. I'll call Jack or the police. I can't have him violate that peace- bond."

Bruce told me she had a recent hysterectomy. She was still healing. She doubted she could leave the house if anything did happen.

"This is just one day," I said. "What comes next?"

"I don't know," she said. "I simply don't know."

I couldn't decide whether to go to his workplace or go straight to the Daly house. I went to his job thinking it might be better to follow him rather than wait. It was a construction site where condos were going up; a high-end part of town with easy access to freeways, malls, restaurants. Good living for those who could afford it.

"He didn't come in today," said his foreman.

"That's odd?" I asked.

"Yeah, he's usually reliable."

"Did he call?" I asked.

"Nope, not a word."

"Is he normally a good worker?"

"Yeah, real good. You give him a shovel and point to a place on the ground, he takes off for China."

I made a dead run for the Daly home. If the kid showed up while I was there, I'd call Jack. That was about all I could do. August Spivey doesn't get between a heated buck and his patch of wool. Not for free.

I pulled up on the Dalys' street, two driveways shy of the Daly house. Two cop cars and an ambulance were parked in front of the house. The nephew's car, a black Nissan pickup, was in the driveway. A lot was happening in the front yard and it didn't look good.

I called Jack on my cell phone. I'd let him call Keri Bruce.

"Jack, give Miss Bruce a call and let her know something big went down. The nephew's truck is here but I don't see him up and moving around. Jack, there's a couple of stretchers and one of them's got a body covered up with a sheet."

I hung up on Jack and moved in closer to the action. The front yard was taped off. Neighbors were gathering. From where I stood, I got a good look at what was going on. One of the stretchers had the covered-up body I told Jack about. The other had a guy with a shirt bloodied-up bad. A woman, and the girl in the photo, were talking to a cop within my earshot.

"He came at my husband. One second they were talking then he lunged at Carl with a knife. He wanted to take Denise with him. We told him to leave. He wouldn't. I shot him with the gun we keep in the bookcase. Look what he did to Carl. Look!"

The daughter stood blank and big-eyed. Maybe she was stunned, maybe she was trying to *look* stunned. The EMS people carried Mr. Daly past me to the ambulance. He had a needle in his arm that led to a bottle full of clear liquid. The way he was knifed made me think the kid went for his throat.

"My own daughter let him in," he said to anybody who would listen. "My own flesh and blood. Chrissake, what's the world coming to?"

4

A DAY IN THE LIFE OF AUGUST SPIVEY

I don't let anything stop me. I don't let my diabetes stop me. I don't let my bipolarity stop me. I don't let my arthritis stop me. You take the average guy, put him in my shoes, my guess is he'd quit. And I've been tempted more than once to suck on the government tit because if anybody can lay claim to disability, I figure it's me. But I keep moving into the future. You can let your problems rise up like a big wall in front of you, or you can throw those problems over your shoulder and carry that load with you, heavy as it is, as you keep on moving. Either way, those burdens ain't going away, so they can beat you or make you stronger.

I get up at four forty-five in the morning. That's my routine. You see, I've got structure. Structure is part of what makes me strong. I'm fifty-eight years old, but in the morning, I feel ninety-eight. That's the way it is. Both my knees hurt, one of them has bone grinding bone. The other one I get shot up once, maybe twice, a year with cortisone. The cortisone has miracle powers. Normally, I drink two cups of coffee black. I read the paper, I move around. My left wrist has arthritis from the psoriasis that plagues me. When the weather's warm, it loosens up in short time. Weather's cold, the wrist hurts like a bitch two or three days at a time.

For breakfast, I eat a big bowl of whole-grain, sugar-free, cheerios with fat-free milk. A couple of years ago I discovered I have the diabetes. The diabetes changed my diet. I was a bacon-and-eggs, biscuits-and-gravy man. I ate what I wanted. Now I don't go near pasta or bread. I'm all about grains and fruits and vegetables. I got to where I couldn't stand the smell of fat-free dressing so I cheat on my salad with the blue-cheese stuff. The problem with the fruits and the vegetables is that they won't fill me up. I can eat a boatload of the healthy food and I'm still hungry. At night, I grill. Normally, I throw chicken or fish on the cooker. Salad, poultry, fish, and fruit; that's a very healthy diet. Sometimes I slip up and throw down a handful of Oreo cookies and a glass of cold, whole milk. God, I miss that. Then I feel guilty and think my arteries are clogging up with all that goo.

I have a deep, internal awareness that the diabetes is a dangerous obstacle to my longevity. It could kill me or drive me into blindness. But like I said, I don't let anything stop me. The diabetes makes me mad. Hard as I work at it, my blood sugar stays higher than what I want. I poke my finger, the sugar's high. Then I think, "What the hell is this about?" My doctor says I'm a *Nervous Nellie*. He tells me I'm a success story because of all the way I've come with my weight and overall health. He tells me to keep doing what I'm doing.

After I wake up thoroughly, I spend time at the computer working on reports. I'm on my third computer in twenty years. I got my first computer by selling my Harley Davidson. I don't know anything about fixing a computer. I can push buttons and create my reports and other paper as long as nothing goes wrong. If something goes wrong, I'm lost.

And I don't call some overseas guy on the phone who can't speak my level of English. I've got my own guy. Rockford had a guy, I've got Torrey. Torrey does some undercover work for me, he delivers lawsuit paper for me, and he's my computer guy. There's nothing about a computer he can't fix. And now he can get me on the phone and take control of my computer by me giving him my IP address. Don't ask me what that means.

My reports have special uniqueness. I built them based on my wealth of experience. My reports have important information about bartenders, cashiers, wait staff, you name it. A waiter doesn't have on his name tag, it's in my report. A waiter doesn't take your drink order as soon as he should, it's in my report. A customer has to wait a long time to get the check, it's in my report. My reports are so good they've been stolen by my competition. Can I prove it? No, but I've got friends in the bar business who showed me reports that have thoughts on them I am certain have come from me. Jack told me to put the copyright on my reports but I wouldn't listen. If I could go back on that, I would. But there's also the factor of my own life experience as a bartender and nobody out there delivers a report of the magnitude and superior knowledge combined into one human being like me.

Normally, I sit down to my computer at seven o'clock in the morning. I have a room in our house dedicated to my business. And that comes in handy at tax time because it is a legitimate business deduction. I work on my reports at least two hours each morning unless I have lawsuit paper to serve in which case I push my reports back into the afternoon. Typically, I get a report out in five days. I like to keep it at 48 hours, but time is a bandit if you're in business for yourself. Most of my clients are hotels. The corporate controllers are the best to deal with. I learned that the hard way. The bar managers and restaurant managers don't hire me. It's them who look bad if I find something wrong. The controllers are the ones who like my work. They are the professionals. They are also polite. But them being bean counters dedicated to numbers and decimal dots, I've got to be prompt and accurate in my thoughts and words. My reports are all of that, and that is why they hire me.

By nine o'clock., I'm ready to exercise. The garage is my favorite room in the house. It's where I go to feel strong. It's where I go to sweat. I sweat out all those psychologic drugs that are supposed to control my anxiety. I said earlier I'm fifty-eight but in the morning when I get up I feel ninety-eight. Well, when I exercise, I feel twenty-eight. I'm loose as a goose for the short while I'm exercising. After two hours in my garage I've got all that missing youth running through my veins. I come out the garage, I'm ready to tear the world a new asshole.

Before I exercise, I tape up. I've got to protect my knees from the possibility they get re-damaged again. I wear a brace on each knee which I reinforce with silver electric tape. NFL quarterbacks don't protect their knees as much as I do. And I dress with the intention to sweat. I've got to sweat. I wear a pair of sweat pants that keeps the heat in around my knees. In the cool months, I wear a sweat shirt over a t-shirt that keeps me pouring out the sweat. And, in the summer when it gets so hot you can't stand it, I still wear a heavy jersey that makes me sweat. All those environmental impurities that poison my body get sent away with my sweat.

First part of my exercise routine is the stretch. I'm not a young colt. I've got to practice patience so I can get my hamstrings and lower back nice and warm. I don't need a sore back or any more leg troubles. I touch my toes while I feel the breath go slowly in and out of me. It also gets my mind into a nice, slow rhythm that makes the total exercise experience one of peace and calm.

When I'm done stretching, I do my stomach work. My doctor tells me belly fat is a chief culprit when it comes to diabetes and disease of the heart area. When I do my sit-ups regularly, it can mean a difference of one or two inches in my belt. That is true. That is fact. Typically, I do thirteen sets of sit-ups, ten sit-ups per set. That's one hundred thirty sit-ups that takes me about twenty minutes to do. I have a bench that sits next to the garage wall where Sandy doesn't park her car. It gives me the surface I need for my sit-ups. Right now, I'm seven pounds over my desirable weight, but it's not because I don't work, it's because of the psychologic drugs that are supposed to calm my unreasonable level of anxiety.

After I cool down from my sit-ups, I jump on the elliptical machine. I never thought I'd like a piece of machinery that has you stand up like you're going up a flight of stairs. Once upon a time, my training was all roadwork. I'd do thirty or forty minutes every day out on the street. But since I tore up my knees, running is out.

I bought the elliptical a year ago at Walmart. I got it for three-hundred bucks which ain't the deluxe model, but it's worked real good so far. I'm not a genius when it comes to machinery, so I pushed the company that manufactured it to come out and do the assembly. The guy had it up and running in no time. I had to get hard with them before they sent their man but sometimes, if you want something, you've got to mean business.

I can jump on the elliptical for 45 minutes. It works my leg muscles, especially above the knees, real hard. It's a good hurt that comes over my legs when I'm on the machine. I've got no cartilage in either knee, so the elliptical is a game-changer for me.

I do another 45 minutes on a recumbent bike that sits between my sit-up bench and the elliptical. A recumbent bike's got a seat that sits at one end of the bike like a chair and has your feet out in front of you. It ain't shaped like a conventional bike. I can change my recumbent into a regular bike if I want but if I sit on a regular bike seat six days a week it feels like I've got a coconut growing out my butt-works.

I close my eyes while I ride the recumbent. Typically, I think about my work, where to make significant changes in my game plan. I also want the time to go by fast since the recumbent can get boring. Both the bike and the elliptical have various levels of difficulty that make me sweat the profuse amounts I like.

By now I've got one hour and forty minutes behind me when you add up the sit-ups, the elliptical, and the recumbent. I am very disciplined when it comes to my workout routine. At this point I drink water from an empty milk jug that holds one gallon of water. I inhale the water like I was in the desert with the sun blazing down on me. Normally, I'll drink half the jug and save the rest for when I finish. The water break takes five minutes. I rest exactly five minutes.

The next station is my body bag. It sits at the end of the garage. I've got a fan that rotates back and forth and bathes the garage in a steady flow of breeze. Jack gave me the punching rig and the bag which is about the size and weight of a grown man.

The bag is my favorite stop in the workout routine. When I work the bag, I allow my imagination to roam. On the elliptical and the recumbent, I get bored, but when I'm hitting the bag, I'm hitting Joe Frazier and George Foreman.

When I was a kid, the heavyweights were my favorite division. All that size and speed and muscle got my attention. Muhammad Ali was my favorite boxer. He made his own rules and didn't let anybody define him.

Boxing is a lonely sport. That's why I like it. It and I identify. I played team sports, and you always had somebody to rely on or they had to rely on you. But in boxing, it's just you and your soul. Sure, you've got a trainer and a manager, but it comes down to taking pain, and giving out pain. It's you reaching into the darkest, deepest part of you and asking yourself what you're willing to go through to win. You run alone, you think alone, but if you can't stand being alone, it ain't for you.

And how do I know this? Because my job is about loneliness. I serve a paper, a hard paper, has some sumbitch avoiding me or putting his burly pit bull on me, I've got to ask myself how important what I do really is.

In my garage, I work the bag for twelve, one-minute rounds. That will wear you out. Between rounds, I take thirty-seconds. So, the bag-work comes to fifteen minutes. I throw about fifty punches a minute. That builds stamina and hand-eye coordination. It also helps me keep my combative edge. I've got no confidence issues when it comes to getting physical with a guy. I'm the complete gentleman, but a guy comes at me with the intention of doing unreasonable harm to my body, I'll put a hand on his face without so much as a worry.

My whole workout comes to one-hundred and twenty-five minutes. I finish off that jug of water, shut off the fan, and go inside. I'm soaked to the skin, so I don't dare sit on any of the inside furniture. We've got some lawn furniture out on our patio so I grab a jumbo tumbler of unsweet iced tea and head out back.

We've got a nice back yard that looks out to a big, open field. A grocery store across a highway tampers a little with the view, but I still get the feel of solitude when

I'm out on the patio. Typically, a breeze that has a clover smell comes across that field. The breeze also cools me down from the workout.

I do some of my best thinking on the patio in the lawn chair after my workout. My mind is clean and calm from the unity of nothing combined with something. That will make sense to those who appreciate a meditative experience. I tried transcendental meditation several times in my life but with my bipolar condition the thoughts don't slow down. Instead, they leave me with what the meditators call a "loud meditation." But with the mindless motion the exercise gives me coupled with the push of oxygen to my brain, I get a ·similar effect which unfortunately is short-lived.

I spend about an hour drying out on the patio then I go inside. Lunch for me consists of fruit and protein. Normally, I take a slice of deli-chicken and sandwich it between a pair of cheddar-cheese slices. I don't use bread. I eat an apple, a banana, and two or three naval oranges. Despite all that fruit and protein, I still have a state of hunger that won't depart. I mix up a glass of low-fat milkshake made specially for diabetics. The shake's got special nutrients that go to the heart of my calorie shortage. The shake gives me a feeling of fulfillment apples or bananas can't match.

Sandy's got a soap opera she's been watching since she was a kid. She and I watch that together. Sometimes I nap, sometimes I watch the plot unwind. I take a hot shower then execute my afternoon. I've got a post office box that sits in a postal substation four miles from the house. First thing I learned in the private-eye business, you've got to remain anonymous. You piss somebody off, you don't want them finding out where you live. For that reason, my phone number is unlisted as well.

The trip to the P.O. box can give me a sense of the productive. Typically, my checks come in sporadically, sometimes three or four weeks after I send out my billing. So, when I open the P.O. box and it's got several checks that total up to a couple thousand dollars, it makes my day. If I've got a paper to deliver or conduct any other business, I do it around my trip to the P.O. box.

I get home, I give the checks to Sandy. Once, I did my own books. Now I let Sandy deal with that. She's responsible with bills, and it takes executive pressure off me which leaves me the time to go out and sell or perform my business. By now, it's about four o'clock in the afternoon, so I give my reports another two hours. That's a total of four hours, two in the morning, and two in the afternoon, I give to my reports. As you can see, I am responsible and disciplined as any corporate guy who goes to work in the morning and comes home at night. I've got more physical risk associated with my business than a guy who works in the corporate sector, but I've also got a freedom most guys don't experience.

At six o'clock, I fire up the grill. Sandy whips up a salad and a vegetable, and we eat out on the patio when the weather is good, or at a table that looks out at our front yard. I go to bed early, usually by eight forty-five. Normally, I fall asleep watching TV in the bedroom. I watch shows that have a mysterious theme. Shows about Big Foot and Loch Ness get my interest. So do shows about visitors from outer space. All the evidence we've got they've been here, the pyramids, and pictures on cave walls of creatures wearing space helmets, I don't see how people can stay closed-minded about visits from beyond.

My favorite shows have ghosts as the subject material. I believe in ghosts with all that is sincere. They've got special recorders on those shows that have ghosts talking and infra-red cameras showing ghost energy walking down halls directly at the camera.

I believe a ghost is a soul that hasn't fully accepted that it is dead. It is a soul in denial it has come from a dead body. When I die, I want to go to Heaven. I don't want to fool around in between the living and the dead. The first anxiety attack I had as a teenage boy, which started all the mental dilemma that plagues me to this day, was me wandering the earth as a tormented soul, crazy out of my mind, not knowing who I am. And I still have bad moments that I could be a ghost condemned to my own personal confusion. You see, I can't face not knowing who I am. I'd rather hate *what* I am, than not know *who* I am.

5

IT'S WHAT I DO

Barnes Wingo hired me. Barnes is a young guy, maybe thirty. I have a lot of respect for Barnes. He's self-made and that goes a long way with me. Some of my pals don't think youth is worth the effort of listening to. I disagree. I've got good rapport with youth. And why wouldn't I? It's their planet too. They're stuck here the same as the rest of us. They'll be the ones who have to live with what's been left behind.

Barnes owns four bars, all of them in Galveston which is driving distance from where Sandy and I live. That makes it very convenient to run down to Galveston, do my bar-work, then come home to the friendly confines of a place that's got no connection to my undercover persona. Plus, I like Galveston. It's an island city with a good number of people, most of them friendly and sun-tanned.

Four times a year I mystery-shop Barnes Wingo's bars. I hit two bars every three months. I've been at it three years for Barnes and it wouldn't surprise me if Barnes stops using me in the near future. Not one time in those three years have I caught one of his bartenders acting outside the ordinary limits of acceptable bartender behavior. By that I mean once in a while I might catch one of the bartenders give a pretty girl a free drink in the hopes of getting close to her, but as a rule his people are honest because of the sweet deal they've got. Barnes pays them good and covers their health insurance so they've got no reason to steal and a hell of a lot to lose if it shows up on my reports that they're in the cookie jar. Rule of thumb: Take care of your hired-help and it won't mess with you. By the way, one thing I won't do is pad my report to make myself look good. And I don't celebrate catching a bartender if he's stealing from the house. But when it happens, I report it the way it is and stand by it all the way through the Employment Commission hearing if it comes to that.

I was working the *Comstock,* the first bar Barnes opened. It's dark with low music, the kind of place an old fart like me can fit in. Barnes's other places aren't too bad to work. Two of them are sports bars, so you get a pretty good mix of people. I can sit at the bar, or at a table nearby, and watch sports, all the time keeping my eye on the bartender. His other place, *Chicken's,* is pure country. When I go in there, I wear cowboy boots and have nothing good to say about the federal government.

A bartender by the name of Meg Jones was behind the bar. You see more women bartenders nowadays then you did back when I was pouring. Once upon a time, it was a man's occupation not counting the lesbian bars, which, needless to explain, usually had a woman behind the bar dressed like a man.

Meg was straight-up honest. No giveaways, no money slipped in her pocket. You run a bar, you want Meg's type on your payroll.

I sat at the bar nursing a Virgin Bloody Mary. Toughest thing for me about mystery-shopping a bartender is watching other people drink. You see, I belong to a group of people that takes life one day at a time, recognizes a higher power, and has a list of twelve things to do.

Normally, I shop a bartender in one-hour blocks. Any longer than that, people get to know me, might figure me out. And I can get to know a lot about a bartender in an hour of undisturbed observation. Typically, I'll do my sitting, then go directly to the men's room where I occupy a stall and make my notes. Private-eye work is about watching and making detailed notes.

I got up to make my bathroom stop when my left leg went out from under me like I had no leg at all. I was on a chair, my foot going to sleep against a metal bar. When I stood, the next thing I knew I was on the floor, all my weight coming down on my left knee cap. Hurt like a sumbitch. I felt the crackle and pop that goes with torn cartilage, or ligaments, or both. The knee buckled immediately, locked-up bad. It felt like I had a cantaloupe where once upon a time was a knee. I've messed up a knee before, that being the other one. I was playing football when my ankle went one direction, my knee collapsing in the other direction. So, I know what it feels like when your knee goes.

I did a little push up then used the bar to pull myself up. Meg came running out from behind the bar, signaling to one of the cocktail waitresses.

"I'm ok," I said.

"What happened?" asked Meg.

"Foot went to sleep."

She and the other girl steadied me for a couple of minutes while a big, black kitchen hand who introduced himself as Ondra helped me out to my car. I took my notes, called Sandy, then took it slow driving home.

The next day my leg wouldn't bend. I laid up on the couch worried sick. I don't walk, I don't work. I kept it packed in ice, took Tylenol, and thought about the steady decline of one August Spivey. I had Sandy call my doctor who said he'd see me in a couple of days.

Two days later I got off the couch. I walked peg-leg, but I could get around. It was my birthday so Sandy and I met Jack at *Chico's*, a Mexican place that has fajitas, beer, and beans so good you'll swear you're done eating white-guy food.

I made my appointment with the doctor then waited on the results of an MRI. Slowly but surely the swelling on my knee went down. I got to where I could bend it a little and walk on it not so stiff-legged. I decided that if I got a call for a mystery-shop or a process-serving job I'd take it.

The MRI came back. It showed the cartilage was torn up badly. The doctor took it nonchalantly; told me I could get it fixed surgically or live with it. I figured long as I could walk and with a periodic shot of cortisone, I'd be all right.

I was in between jobs, doing what I do when I don't have work. I drove around town, checked my P.O. box, waited on edge for the phone to ring. After a week of driving Sandy nuts, the phone rang. It was Neal Green's office wanting me to serve a Mexican fellow by the name of Gutierrez.

Neal and I usually don't talk directly. Once upon a time we got along fine, but with both of us prone to blowing up, we keep it minimal.

I stopped by his office and picked up the paper from his paralegal, Julietta Rojas. Julietta's a Mexican girl. She speaks English and Mexican fluently. She and I work well together. She grew up locally, graduated from one of the public schools, and put herself through paralegal school. A good amount of Neal's work involves Mexicans suing Mexicans, so him having Julietta was no accident. Since I've been delivering lawsuit paper for Neal, all but one of his girls have been Mexican.

Gutierrez lived in a manufactured home that looked like it fell out of the sky. It sat crooked on a lot in a rundown trailer park with high weeds, rusty cars on blocks, and junk scattered everywhere. Why people hang onto their junk I don't understand. You can't sell it, you can't give it away, and it has no use unless you've got a soft spot in your heart for rats.

Gutierrez' yard was fenced, a white-picket square in bad need of paint and nails. That told me he might have a dog. A beat-up Dodge pickup was parked to the left of a set of wooden stairs that had a couple of planks missing and led to a wooden porch. On the porch sat a pair of aluminum deckchairs on each side of a storm-door.

I opened the gate, shook my keys, then limped cautiously toward the stairs. Each step I took hurt. I put most of my weight on my other bad knee which was now my good knee. I stopped at the bottom of the stairs. The pickup was behind me about five feet away on a driveway that ran past the fence onto the street. Once upon a time there were five steps leading up to the porch. Two were missing, the third and fourth, leaving me a good look under the house, a dark place with a wet smell. With my knee screaming at me I climbed the stairs, stepping over the missing boards. I walked to the door and knocked. No one answered. I put my card in the door then stepped carefully, going back down the stairs. I heard a low growl come from under the truck. Not a little-dog growl, but something from a nightmare that would freeze you up inside. I walked backwards, careful not to trip over the old tires and other crap that made up most of the front yard.

That night I nursed my knee with cold packs. I made notes about my first attempt at personal service on Gutierrez. Typically, I make three bonafide attempts to put paper in the guy's hand. After that, I build my affidavit for substitute service. I got up the next morning and limped through my morning ritual of a shower and shave. I was hurting too much to exercise in my garage. I ate light. I made another run to Gutierrez' house, playing it carefully with whatever animal was under the truck. Like the first attempt, the stairs were a bitch and no one answered the door. This time, no sound came from under the truck.

My third time out was two days later. I'd rather serve a guy personally, put paper in his hand, and then wish him luck and move on. You get into the area of substitute service, the due process part of my job comes into question. But when a guy avoids, and it came apparent Gutierrez was avoiding, sometimes you've got no choice.

I pulled up to Gutierrez' home, walked to the gate, then did my little ritual with the keys. I've had dogs come running at the sound of those keys. I heard nothing at the bottom of the stairs which left me feeling good and bad. Not all dogs growl. Some will sneak up on you. I knocked on Gutierrez' front door for the third and last time. I'd make my notes, enter them into affidavit form, then give it to Julietta who would get a court-ordered notice of suit that I would place on Gutierrez' front door. I would also charge one-hundred and fifty dollars for my work. Normally, I charge fifty, but when I have go back to establish my three attempts, time can turn into money.

Bottom of the stairs I heard what I didn't want to hear. That jungle growl from before came out from under the truck. I backed up slowly, a yellow note pad and the civil process in my right hand. Unlike the first time I heard the growl, this one was closer to the bumper which put the animal near my right leg. Five feet from the truck, me backing up, it charged.

It was a pit bull; grey, pissed off, its teeth wet and sharp. I've got a good buddy who once raised pits for all the wrong reasons. I don't consider him an expert, but he's a smart guy who likes to research the things he does. He tells me that 65% the attacks on people by dogs are done by pits. A pit, he says, has no red light in its psychology. Bred to kill, they lock down on you, they don't know how to let go.

I back-peddled, the pit on me in two leaps. With the yellow legal pad, I slapped it on the snout. If I tripped, I'd be on the ground, it's jaws on my leg or, God help me, my throat. I felt no pain in my knee. My heart was beating like a tom-tom. Those legs that two-seconds ago were fifty-eight years old now belonged to a teenage kid. The pit came hard, growling, snapping, until the chain leash he was on snapped him into a backflip.

I rested in my car with sweat beading up on my forehead. The pit was in the yard, its leash pulled tight, five or six feet from the gate. My guess was that Gutierrez had kept his dog under the truck, maybe with one of the wheels parked on top of the leash so the pit could growl, but not get out in the open. With me trying continuously to get him served, Gutierrez gave the pit enough chain to chase me down.

I looked into the yard and realized I dropped the civil process a few inches from where the animal was pulling tight on the chain and growling at me low, mean and steady. I needed the paper. I went back in the yard, with my left knee locked up, the pit going crazy. I looked for something to reach with, grabbed an old radio antenna, then pulled the paper my way. I bent over slowly, grabbed it, heat and spit from the dog's muzzle touching my hand.

At the house, I calmed down with a cold shower. I wanted a drink badly, but if I drink one, I'd drink an ocean. The shower did the trick, otherwise I was on the phone to my sponsor.

I slept like a rock, something I hadn't done in years. All that adrenaline that had gone through me, once it was gone, I was beat. My head hit the pillow at eight o'clock and I didn't open my eyes until six the next morning. The way I felt was a blessing. What I would give to sleep like that every night!

Next morning the knee was killing me but I pushed myself to call Julietta. An hour later I dropped off my affidavit for substitute service.

"I ain't going back in that yard, Julietta. I made my three attempts. And I'm not posting the notice on the front door."

"I understand," she said.

That afternoon she had the notice ready for posting. Typically, I post notice of substitute service on the front door in a clear plastic glove so no way the recipient can say he didn't get it.

"Post it on the window of his car," said Julietta. "Neal says as long as it's obvious, it should work."

I drove straight out to Gutierrez' house, thinking along the way maybe I'd done damage to my knee running backwards from the pit. Gutierrez had another car, a blue El Camino he parked on the apron of the driveway on the street side of the fence. I had an easy time taping the plastic envelope with the notice of service visible on the back window of the car.

Two mornings later, I got a bad call from Julietta.

"Augie, you gotta go back."

"Why?" I asked.

"Judge Toomey won't accept the service. Said the car is mobile; said it could be anybody's car; said he wants something more substantial before he signs his order granting service."

"I ain't going in the yard, Julietta."

"I know, Augie. I know."

My wife Sandy's comfortable in the wilderness. You put her in the woods, she can take care of herself. Me, I hate the woods. I'm an urban boy who likes ballgames, movies, and restaurants. I don't eat bark and I don't wipe my ass with pine cones.

I asked Sandy to go along with me. She's good at rigging things, a holdover from her camping days, and if Gutierrez showed himself, an extra person along might discourage him if he wanted violence. Process servers who get attacked are usually working solo when they get it. And if Gutierrez gave his dog enough leash to come after me, I didn't trust him far as I could throw a truck.

When we got to Gutierrez' house, the dog was nowhere in sight. The Ford pickup was gone. Sandy fastened the notice to the front gate with enough tape to hold a horse. Only way Gutierrez could miss it would be if he grew wings and went into the house at night through a hole in the roof.

A week later Julietta called me with news Judge Toomey accepted the substitute service I placed on the gate. She thanked me for my work, and said I could expect my check for $150 in the mail.

"Julietta, I'm tired of dogs. No more dogs. You hear me?"

"They come with the territory, Augie. You don't want the tough jobs, Neal says we don't need you for any of the jobs."

I told her to keep the work coming, dogs included. I laid low for a couple of days nursing the knee which got a little better. Sandy and I have a patio in the back yard that looks out at a field. I rested on a recliner, watching the sun go down. Years ago, if you asked me to look into the future and see where I was now I'd take it, despite this crazy-ass job, because my life worked out better than I expected. It's what I do.

6

THE BROTHERS SPIVEY

Sometimes you gotta get dirty. Sometimes you go places, do things, that make you wonder if you're in the right line of work.

I took a job from a bar owner by the name of Bobby Truax. Two and two being four, I figured Bobby for queer. Bobby dressed like a man, smoked cigarettes like a man, had a queer girl's haircut.

But she was married to a guy about half her forty years and they had a kid. Her husband looked as queer as her, but if the little girl between them was for real, then somewhere along the way hubby's inner-man connected with Bobby's inner-woman.

Bobby owned three bars. Two of them, *Big* and *True,* I'd spent my share of quality time in. The third one, *Trotsky's,* I wouldn't go near. If anyplace sounds "commie," I won't drink there. I don't need the world thinking I'm pink.

Bobby and I found each other in the Yellow Pages. We had a warm little phone-chat, her telling me she had a bartender stealing from her, me telling her that once upon a time I was a bartender, twenty years of it. If a bartender blinks wrong, I can spot it.

So, Bobby Truax and I sat down at *Trotsky's* (of all places) to see how I could help her out.

"Oh, she's stealing from me. I know that much," said Truax.

"You seem sure."

"I'm very sure."

"Something tells me you had an audit that didn't turn out so good."

And that's where I figured she and I tied our own, *'until-death-do-us-part,'* business-knot. You see, her being a bar owner, me a reformed bartender, we both knew the drill. It works something like this: whiskey goes out, money comes in. End of the month, money's supposed to equal whiskey. Every bartender spills, every bartender breaks a bottle here and there. And every now and then, a drink gets given away to a good-looking woman seated at the bar maybe the bartender wants to meet later. All that gets factored in. But when the state does an audit, (and it does, regularly, because it wants its piece of the action too), and every drop of your whiskey over the spills, the breaks, and the giveaways talks to you and says, *"Hey Mr. Bar Owner, somebody's been letting me go out the door, not giving you your money. You got to pay your bills. You got to pay your whiskey taxes. You got to live. You got a wife who likes nice things. You got your own taste for life. Can't do that if somebody's stealing,"* then you have a problem that only I can solve.

Any bartender who stands upright can figure out how to skim the house. Bottom line, if a bartender keeps his theft in an acceptable fudge-area, he flies under the radar, everybody stays happy, and the bar owner probably leaves him alone.

So how does a bartender steal? He games the register. A couple times a night he'll walk over to the register, open the drawer, put money in just like an honest man. Only he doesn't ring the register. He *pretends* like he rings the register. If he's seasoned at all, each time he puts a bill in, say a Jackson, he breaks off a piece of a toothpick, puts that broken piece of wood into a glass he keeps safe in a place that he comes back to at closing. Then he counts his toothpicks; he knows how many Jacksons to take out of the register he's been so nice to. He does that just a little bit here and there, he takes away maybe a hundred a week. That's four hundred a month. He does that every other month, and he gets away with it. Problem is, maybe he gets a little greedy. It starts to get too easy. Maybe he's got a spoiled girlfriend, high on the maintenance, who likes to eat out at those places you got to call ahead to if you want a table. Maybe he's got his eye on a Jaguar a guy like him's got no business dreaming about. Or maybe he's a lonely boy, wants a regular, pay-for-it, piece of ass.

A bartender named Connie Sikma was doing the stealing. Things worked out real good at first. Truax gave her good money, made her manager of *Trotsky's*. Truax started spending more time away with her husband and kid. A year or so ago, Sikma wanted a buy-in. Truax wasn't in a sharing mood.

"Bitch stole over ten thousand from me and had the nerve to try to buy into my business. How stupid does she think I am?"

Her voice went a little flimsy. I gave her a minute to calm down. She might've looked like a guy, deep down in her girlie-works wanted *to be* a guy, but when it came crying-time, I got the impression she could misty-up with any woman.

"Couple of other things."

"What's that?" I asked.

"Her boyfriend's a guy owns several bars here in town. Mickey Tiger. You know him?"

"Yeah, I do," I said. "I've done work for him. Small world, ain't it?"

"So, he knows you? "

"I doubt he remembers me. This Sikma, she's an older lady?"

"Oh no," said Truax. "She comes in about forty, easy to look at."

I kept my unruly trap shut while Bobby Truax read my simple mind.

"Look, when it comes to my bars, I'm all business. This is about her stealing from me. And if my money ends up somehow in one of Mickey Tiger's bars, you've never seen crazy."

"There was something else?" I asked.

"Yeah, Mickey Tiger fucked her on one of my pool tables."

"How do you know that?"

"I got a phone call. Anonymous. I know the voice, but I can't place it. Same voice that told me she was stealing from me."

"Be very nice if you could remember who this was."

"I know, you don't have to tell me."

"You think it's somebody who worked for you?"

"No, I'd figure that out. It's somebody who came in, maybe regular, to one of my bars. I can't put the voice with a face."

"He saw her steal?"

"So he says."

"And he saw the action on the pool table?"

"Yeah. Connie and some others partied after hours. People got drunk. Mickey had her on one of those."

Truax pointed to a pair of pool tables that took up a lot of good drinking space. "A sixty-five-year-old guy, out in the open, people watching."

I told her the best thing for me to do was get a good look at Connie Sikma in action. *Trotsky's* was standard honky-tonk: smoke, big-screen TV, pool tables, loud guys hitting on easy bar wool. Close up, Connie Sikma looked good enough to satisfy most guys, and give an old man like Mickey Tiger a happy heart attack. She ever walked the aisle with Mickey, she'd have people pouring suds for her one day.

People might think bartenders are nothing but glorified beer jocks. They couldn't be more wrong. A pro can mix eighty drinks from memory, all the time he's handling money, making small-talk with the pretty girls. When I was pouring, I got to where I could spot an undercover guy just by the way he sat at the bar. Guy comes in, he's not a regular, doesn't watch any TV, he doesn't try to pick up women, he just sits there sipping so slow at his beer it gets warm. You don't have to be a white guy on "Tejano" night for a bartender to figure you out.

Saturday's a good night to spot. Crowd's usually good, bartender doesn't have time to notice who's watching. My line of bullshit had me dumped by a cougar wife who traded up for a kid with money. Sikma was a little weak on the pour, but smooth as silk when it came to sweet-talking the thirsty and the sad. I told her this brave new world of singledom had me all messed up. She threw some sympathy my way, I tipped her good.

Trotsky's had a pair of registers that made the money trail a trip through time and space. One register acted like a register should. It opened, it shut, it took cash. It sat lonely on a service bar that wasn't part of the regular action. The one that got all the attention was parked near Sikma. It took cash, but the register tape had died and gone to Heaven.

Way it worked, Sikma did business on the broken register. End of the night, she made one big ring on the good register. Only person who used either register was Connie Sikma. On that, Bobby Truax made it clear. Sikma

42

alone held the keys. Two registers, one bartender, Connie Sikma.

I sat down on her for two hours. I rolled in at ten, stayed until midnight. The bar was three sides of a rectangle, one long side, two short. I put myself on a short side with a good look at the busted register that sat about fifty feet away. From there Sikma couldn't go to the register without me seeing her. Nowadays, I'd catch her being naughty on a tiny camera that sits in my pocket, looks like a pencil. Back then, it was eyeballs, memory, and a tape recorder I kept in the car.

Sikma had been bartending three years, all for Truax. She came right out of bartending school, same as me when I was in the trade. Bartending school teaches you the drinks, how to carry yourself. It's a faster way to good money than learning on the job. One thing bartending school doesn't teach you is how to steal. If you've never been spotted, if you don't know how to spot a spotter, you make rookie mistakes. Out of the chute, Sikma was putting money, lots of it, in her shirt pocket. Tip jars were doing just fine which told me she was holding money with a register close enough that she could touch it.

I left the bar thinking I needed a look-see at her bar tabs. In my truck, I made a short, verbal report on a hand-held recorder I kept in the glove box. I always fill out my report later based on my taped report. I use it to keep things fresh. I don't skip any detail when I record: the date, the time, what the bartender wore, his name tag, his age, his build. I want no doubt about who I'm watching. And I don't want a guy fired if he gets mixed up with some other bartender because I made a poor report.

I went to a *Denny's* not far from *Trotsky's*. The bar closed at two and I needed to kill some time. A waitress took my order. She looked older than she was, and tired. It made me think the whole world was tired. Tired of itself. I saw that tired world in her face. A face that asked why the hell she spread her legs for some guy who didn't care about her, who left her with kids at home. The only way to be a good parent was to be a great parent.

You watch private eye television, you get guns and girls. Guys like me, the small timers, you sit, you worry, you wonder if it all comes together good enough that you make your client happy. And you get dirty. Sometimes it's garbage, sometimes it's the ugly side of man. But you get dirty.

At two-thirty, I got dirty. I started sifting through garbage on the backside of *Trotsky's* with a pair of latex gloves and a set of barbecue tongs. I went through garbage bags big as me that held all sorts of human goo. I went through garbage bags big as me that held things a rat wouldn't touch. I went through garbage bags big as me that held girlie-napkins, Kleenex, toilet paper, stuff you don't tell your wife about if you want back in the house again. And I found those tabs, for I was blessed.

I changed T-shirts at my truck then threw the dirty shirt, the latex gloves, and the barbecue tongs into a paper grocery bag. I put the receipts into a plastic baggy. At home, I undressed in the garage, threw my clothes into the washing machine, then showered. I scrubbed hard enough, long enough, if I was a dark man I'd have turned white. Sandy knew I'd be getting dirty. I prepared her for it. She was sound asleep when I got home. I crawled into bed at seven in the morning and slept like a baby until noon. I woke up thinking about my dip in the shit river. For breakfast, I had an orange juice, a black coffee, and a glass of Sandy's filtered water. The only stuff going into me for a while would be cold, clean, or boiled and wouldn't remind me of that dumpster.

The tabs gave me what I wanted. I read them in the garage on a table that sits in the corner. I counted forty tabs, if there were more, they got away. Every tab had a drink total: five Lone Stars here, four Margaritas there. Sales were heavy on beer, light on the mixed drinks. There were twenty-five tabs with nothing but beer. Fifteen tabs showed mixed drinks or, part mixed drinks and part beer. Some of the beer tabs had hash marks in the upper right corner.

I culled the tabs with the hash marks, set them to the left, then put the rest of the tabs into their own pile. I counted all the drinks on all the tabs, counted the hash marks, came up with one-hundred twenty-five drinks sold and twenty-five hash marks. Bottom line, at closing, Sikma should've entered at least one-hundred-twenty-five drinks in the good register.

Trotsky's was closed Sunday and Monday. I called Truax, told her to check the good register tape as of 2 am. I kept quiet on the number of drinks that should've been rung. I wanted Truax to read me the numbers. The number she came back with put a smile on the mug of Augie Spivey. At closing, Sikma rang one-hundred drinks. Twenty-five drinks, all beers, never got rung. Do a little arithmetic, figure the price of the beers, Sikma skimmed about a hundred dollars. I had to think the money that went in her pocket was the money didn't make it into the good register.

Did Sikma steal ten thousand dollars of Bobby Truax's money over the last two years? I don't know. I know I nailed her thieving ass one soon-to-be-special night out of her life. My work wouldn't beat reasonable doubt, but it wasn't a criminal charge I was after. If it came down to *just cause,* I could meet that burden if Truax wanted to dump Sikma and not pay her unemployment insurance. Bottom line, Truax didn't need my report to fire Sikma.

Past the unemployment payout, I figured she wanted something to waive in Sikma's face for the pure pleasure of it.

I built my report around my taped notes, my first-hand look at Connie Sikma behind the bar, and the receipts I pulled from the trash. As part of my file, I kept photocopies of the tabs. I gave the originals back to Bobby Truax. I put the bar tabs and my report in a nice brown envelope then mailed it off.

We talked on the phone two days later, me making sure she got the report. She let me know she let Connie Sikma go. I asked her how it went, she said it wasn't pretty. There was the weeping and gnashing of teeth. She asked me to remind her what she owed me. I told her I'd follow with my written bill, but with time being money, I couldn't help but come in at least twenty hours when you figured in my time perched on a bar-stool, my phone visits with her, and a night spent in the trash. She said she'd follow with a check in the mail if it was acceptable to me. To that I was agreeable.

Next few days, Sandy and I took it easy. I had a grand coming, my mood was as good as it gets. I decided a break from the rigors of private investigation was in order. We went out to lunch twice, caught a bargain movie, and stopped at a pair of used car lots, me thinking I'd need a fresh ride pretty soon. Before the check came in, I got a bad, but expected, call.

"It's a game-changer," I said, "but I saw it coming. Didn't you?"

"Yeah, I guess I did," said Truax, "she has nothing to lose."

The chit-chat between me and Bobby Truax wasn't cozy, but being business people we kept it professional. Connie Sikma wasn't taking it laying down. She filed for unemployment with the state employment commission. Bobby Truax came back just as hard. No way that she-bitch was going to squeeze more money from her.

"What about a lawyer? Will I need one?"

"Yeah," I said, "it wouldn't hurt."

My brother Jack lawyers for a bank. Long as he's done that, he says he's never had a boring day. Jack pushes paper. He closes land deals, negotiates mortgages, gives advice to the higher-ups in his bank. Every now and then he forecloses on a family farm, work I know he hates. You take away Mr. Green-jeans, Jack's job is mostly paper, phone calls, and other property lawyers.

Jack's been in a courtroom a couple of times. He's done a few "no-contest" divorces for family and friends. Anything Jack does in a courtroom he does pro bono on the trade-off that whoever he helps accepts the outcome with no pissing or moaning because he'll give you his best for free.

Jack went sour on pro bono a few years ago. He helped a twelve-year-old kid in a custody suit. The kid wanted away from her mamma, a very bad girl when it came to sex, drugs, and rock n roll. Things got a little nasty. Jack got custody of the child switched over to the ex, then a year later, about the time her woman-sap started running, the kid went back to mamma. Nowadays, Jack's more careful about who he helps.

Jack and I see life as something you can't trust. The way we deal with it is another matter. Jack figures things being crazy, you can't be too careful. My view, you may as well jump in and have your fun. All comes out about the same, right?

Our old man was mostly Irish; our mother a German girl from the Midwest. Both my dad's brothers married Midwest Germans. Me, Jack, our three sisters and two big families of cousins are all Irish-German. You go to a Spivey reunion, half of us stay up drinking, singing, and waiting for the rooster to crow. The other half hit the sack early, worrying the world is pulling apart.

"Jack, I'll get to the point. You like it when I do that, don't you?"

I called Jack at work, knowing if it was him, and not his secretary who picked up the phone, he'd give me a few minutes of his precious time.

"Yeah Augie, I like it that way."

I went into a little ta-ta-ta about how Connie Sikma was robbing Bobby Truax blind; how I'd spent a night wading through the used-up side of man, about my ongoing struggle with the world, a world that did nobody any favors, how he and I had to claw our way up, trying to make some sense of this crazy, fucked-up lump of dirt floating around in space, and now, for the first time in my self-made life, I had a chance, a big chance, to take the big step, to have it all come together, if I could just get the serious attention of one Bobby Truax.

"Get to the point, Augie."

"Jack, I'm so close to my ship coming in. But I need you."

When Jack wears his lawyer's hat he listens hard, interrupts when he wants, says that's how he wraps his mind around the problem on the table.

"Boy, Augie, I don't know. That's a lot of work. I've got to study the Administrative Code, teach myself how their hearings go. Whole new set of rules with those people. Evidence is different. And then there's taking time off from my work. My job is important. We closed a billion in loans last year. My phone rings a lot. We're talking about a large pain in the ass here, Augie."

"Jack, I wouldn't call you if I wasn't on the doorstep of something important. It was you who said, 'You can do the little things, the right way, that make a difference or you can do tired, stupid things that invite failure.' You said that, Jack. I remember. Gospel!"

"I don't know, Augie."

"Jack."

"What, Augie?"

"Please?"

This time we got together at Bobby Truax's house, a southwestern style place with a pool in a part of town you had to make good money to live in. Jack, Bobby Truax and I sat out by the pool while the husband and the kid splashed around in the water.

"She worked five nights a week, managed, bartended, and I paid her damn good."

"But she didn't get sick or take a vacation?" asked Jack.

"Sure, she took a week of vacation. She took a day or two of sick leave. I paid her for both. Somebody works for me a year, they get a week of vacation and a week of sick, paid."

"And who covered for her when she was gone?"

"Me."

"Respectfully, Ms. Truax, but couldn't you have taken the money?"

"Sure, I'd steal from myself. I love looking like an idiot."

"This guy who called you on the phone and said Sikma was stealing from you, you think maybe one of your bartenders was trying to shift blame over to her?"

"Anything's possible, but the money all came out of *Trotsky's*. It didn't come out of my other places, just *Trotsky's*. And it's all happened since she hired on. I have gone over and over that conversation a dozen times and for the life of me, I can't place the voice. But it's not any of my other bartenders. It's driving me nuts. You think we should bring up her and Mickey Tiger on the pool table?"

"If we could prove it," said Jack. "But without that guy who called you, all we have is Augie's work, which is good, but is at best circumstantial. It's a long-shot."

"I'll pay you for your work," said Truax. "I'm not looking for a free ride."

"Let's do this," said Jack. "I'll work this pro bono. We'll call it part of your deal with Augie. Win or lose, you take a fair look at Augie down the road."

A pair of hours went by real quick. Jack did what he does. He listened, he interrupted, he explained how evidence in an employment hearing was more relaxed than in a regular court room. If you lost, you could file a fresh lawsuit in district court. If it came to that, she'd have to get another lawyer. District court wasn't Jack's kind of rodeo.

"The burden of proof is on you to make it clear and convincing to the hearing examiner that she took the money and she did it intending to steal. Basically, I have to get into the examiner's head, make him see it our way. Her lawyer will be doing the same thing, same issues, but trying to counter what we're trying to do."

We left it there, Jack driving home the point that unless we came up with the mystery phone caller it was a battle uphill. If she was OK with that, we'd go forward, none of us backing down.

Day of the hearing we met in a building that had a pair of rooms so cozy you could smell each other's habits. Sikma's lawyer was a stalwart bitch named Gretchen Mueller. I knew Gretchen, Jack did too. I served paper for Gretchen. God willing, I'd work for her again. Jack knew her through legal circles. Gretchen was as round as a tent, and out to make the world pay for the loneliness written all over her. Jack tried to make small talk with her, but when Gretchen went on the clock, she was the fifth face on Rushmore.

Everybody knew everybody one way or another, a little or a lot. It made me wonder why the hell a lawsuit was going on. Jack and Gretchen both knew the hearing examiner, John Krupa. Mickey Tiger didn't know me personally, but he and I had done business. Bobby Truax and Connie Sikma wouldn't look at each other. Far as they were concerned, that said plenty. And Mickey and Bobby had both been crossing paths for years in the bar world. I've been to baptisms where the people weren't this close.

Inside the hearing we took chairs around a big table that took up most the room. John Krupa introduced himself, set down the rules, and warned us we had to keep things nice and polite.

Jack led off with me. He handed copies of my report and the state liquor audit to Gretchen Mueller and Krupa.

"What is important about the hash marks?"

"They're a good way to count drinks," I said.

"And why would you want to count them?"

"So you can know how many drinks don't get rung up in your register. It's how you steal."

"You watched Connie Sikma bartend, correct?"

"Correct."

"And what did you see ?" asked Jack.

"I saw her put money, several times, in her breast pocket."

"Several times?"

"Ten times," I said.

Jack and I walked through my night at *Trotsky's*, what I found in the garbage, the story the tabs told.

"There were forty tabs," I said. "You look at the tabs with hash marks, you'll see twenty-five hash marks. You look at the register tapes tagged onto my report, compare what was sold to what got rung up, you'll see twenty-five drinks didn't get rung into the register at the end of the night."

"It says on the state audit," said Jack, "that missing from *Trotsky's* over the last two years were ten thousand dollars in liquor sales. Would you say Connie Sikma stole that much?"

"I wouldn't know," I said.

"But what do you know?" asked Jack.

"That she put money in her pocket ten times, that there were twenty-five hash marks on bar tabs, that twenty-five drinks didn't get recorded."

"Mr. Spivey, how do you know so much about bartending?"

"I bartended for twenty years."

"So, you know the tricks a bartender uses when he or she steals?"

"I do."

"Have you ever stolen from a bar owner?"

"No."

"Have you ever turned in another bartender who you knew was stealing?"

"You mean, when I was bartending?"

"Yes," said Jack.

"No, I didn't," I said. "It's part of my 'don't steal, don't squeal' policy."

It was time for Gretchen Mueller to take a bite out of me. The work I'd done for her in the past was top-notch. I figured as long as I was respectful, she'd use me again. But today, I was just another guy sitting in a chair saying nasty things about her client.

"You weren't in the bar at closing, correct?" she asked.

"Correct."

"So you didn't see Connie Sikma leave the bar with any money, did you?"

"No but..."

"You didn't see Connie Sikma leave the bar with any money, did you?"

"No, but like I ...."

"You didn't see Connie Sikma leave the bar with any money, did you?"

"No, I didn't," I said.

Jack came back with a few questions of his own.

"Do you think she might have thrown the money in the garbage?" he asked.

"No," I said.

"You think she might have lit a match to the money, burned it up?"

"No," I said.

"You think maybe she drew those hash marks because she likes to put little stick-men on pieces of paper?"

"I doubt it," I said.

The hearing went like a prizefight, my boy, Jack, bobbing and weaving. He took a few to the chin, but he threw a few back. Jack wasn't bad on his feet, but it was Gretchen Mueller who court-roomed for a living. Done with me, Jack passed on Bobby Truax, waiting to use her for rebuttal. It was Connie Sikma's turn. It didn't surprise me that she came across like honey and butter on warm bread.

"So you put money in your pocket?" asked Mueller.

"Yes, I did," said Sikma.

"Why would you do that?"

"It's convenient. I hate running back and forth to the register, especially on a busy night. Look, I'm a little lazy. I admit it. But I'm not a thief."

"And the hash marks?"

"Same answer. It lets me keep money in my pocket so at the end of the night I'll know how much to put in the register from my pocket, not take it out."

"Now, Miss Sikma, you are aware of an audit conducted by the state?"

"I am."

"And you know it found in excess of ten thousand dollars missing from *Trotsky's* over the last two years?"

"I am."

"What do you say to that?"

"I'm shocked. I don't know how to react to that. But it hurts because I love *Trotsky's*. I hope they catch whoever took it if it was stolen."

I knew she was lying, but I had to hand it to her, she looked pouty and hurt and even I wanted to believe her. Bobby Truax was staring nails at Sikma. She leaned into Jack and whispered.

"Are you going to push her about the pool table?"

"No, we can't prove it. You want to look foolish or desperate, bring that up without any proof."

Gretchen Mueller asked Sikma.

"You were a good employee?"

"Yes, I was."

"Did you show up for work, regularly, on time?"

"Yes, I did."

"Did you ever abuse your vacation or sick leave?"

"No, I was very responsible about the job."

"And you worked hard?"

"Yes."

"So, why would Miss Truax insist that you stole from her?"

"Well, I have a suspicion, but it's difficult to talk about it."

"Take your time. Tell us."

"It's …it's embarrassing."

"That's OK. You don't have to be embarrassed here. We're trying to get to the truth."

"I rejected her."

"In what way?"

"She put hands on me."

"What do you mean?"

"I mean she came up behind me and…."

"Then what happened?" asked Mueller.

"She fondled me."

"How so?"

"She touched me inappropriately."

"Please explain."

"She put her hands on my behind. Oh my, I can't talk about this."

"That's OK. Nobody here is judging you."

"She came around my front, with her hands."

"Yes."

"And then, well, she held my breasts."

"Did you tell her to stop?"

"I wiggled free. That was my way of telling her to leave me be."

"What did she do?"

"She didn't say anything. She walked away."

"How were things after that?"

"Not the same."

"You could have quit, gotten a lawyer, complained through proper legal channels. Why didn't you?"

"No," said Sikma, "I had nowhere to go, so I let it go."

"Miss Sikma?"

"Yes."

"Did you steal from *Trotsky's*?"

"No."

"Have you ever stolen anything from Miss Truax?"

"No."

Bobby Truax leaned again into Jack.

"Unbelievable lying bitch," she said

It was Jack's turn to work over Connie Sikma. I didn't imagine him taking any prisoners.

"You kept money in your pocket and drew hash marks on bar tabs because it was convenient?"

"Yes."

"In a sense, you were the cash register, correct?"

"I'm not sure I follow."

"You held the money, you recorded the sales."

"Well, I guess that's one way to look at it."

"Did Bobby Truax know you did that?"

"No."

"Why?"

"Well, she wouldn't approve of it."

"She did, in fact, have a rule against that sort of thing?" asked Jack.

"Yes."

"So you knowingly violated your employer's cash-control policy, correct?"

"Yes, I did."

"You did that regularly?"

"No, just...."

Jack interrupted, "Just the night twenty-five drinks didn't get into the register."

Connie Sikma held serve. She kept a steady look, but inside, I bet she felt like she just ate a boiled rat.

"Now, after you were allegedly groped by Bobby Truax, you had nowhere to go."

"That is correct."

"That must have been tough, staying there, after being humiliated. She could have very easily groped you again."

"It was very difficult."

"But you had no choice. Couldn't get a lawyer. Had no legal recourse. You had to swallow your pride because you had no place to go."

"I've already said that."

"But you really did have a choice, didn't you?" asked Jack.

"I don't know what you mean."

"You have a boyfriend, true?"

"Yes."

"And he was your boyfriend when the groping took place?"

"Yes."

"And he owns how many bars?"

"I don't know."

I peek-a-booed Mickey Tiger. He looked mad enough, if he took a piss, he could put out the sun.

"I can answer that," he said.

"No, I want Miss Sikma to answer," said Jack.

"This is between Mr. Spivey and Miss Sikma," said Krupa.

"Would you like me to tell you how many bars he owns?" asked Jack.

"If you like," said Sikma.

"He owns six. Did you know that?"

"I suppose I did," said Sikma.

"And you had no place to go?"

Next up was Bobby Truax. She had a look in her eye that said she was a cobra and Connie Sikma was a mouse.

"Miss Truax, did you grope Connie Sikma?"

"No."

"Have you ever groped anybody?"

"No."

"Then why would Miss Sikma say you did?"

"Because she's a liar. Because she stole from me. Because her back's up against the wall."

You could've put ice on Bobby Truax's forehead and it wouldn't have melted. The way she held herself told me she had nothing to be ashamed of.

"Do you have an ax to grind with Connie Sikma?"

"Other than her stealing from me, no."

"How do you know she stole from you?"

"The state audit didn't lie. Then there's the private eye's report. Any talk about me stealing from myself or another bartender taking that kind of money is nonsense. She stole from me. I have no doubt about it. She may get away with it, but she stole a boatload of money from me."

Gretchen Mueller passed on Truax. Jack summarized, pointing to the state audit and my report. Bottom line, Connie Sikma stole from *Trotsky's* the night I was there and that's all was needed to cut her off from unemployment. Gretchen Mueller came back with her own bottom line; nobody saw Connie Sikma steal anything.

John Krupa turned off the tape recorder then gave the room a minute to settle down. He explained that we'd get a decision in the mail in about six weeks. He thanked us for our time, told us we could leave.

Outside the hearing room Jack, Bobby Truax and I huddled. Gretchen Mueller and Connie Sikma walked by.

Jack and Gretchen Mueller nodded at each other. I winked at Gretchen Mueller. I had future business with her to consider. Bobby Truax tried to make hard-eyes with Connie Sikma, but Sikma was memorizing the floor.

"What did you make of what she said about me?" asked Truax.

"The harassment?" asked Jack.

"Yeah."

"I assume you were truthful with me?"

"I was," said Truax.

"That's good to know," said Jack. "I like being right about the people I'm supposed to believe in."

Bobby Truax cut me a check on the spot. I doubted I'd see her again.

"Jack," I said later in the car, "admit it. In that hearing room, you've never felt more alive."

Six weeks later Jack got the news from John Krupa that Connie Sikma would be getting her unemployment insurance. I boohooed about losing Bobby Truax, not to mention Mickey Tiger, as my customer.

"Truax got a good deal," said Jack. "You outted a thief. And she got my best lawyering for free. Time to move on."

Next couple of months, I phoned Jack several times, but he wouldn't return my calls. He probably thought I wanted another favor. Jack's got a saying that goes, "Some people are like cats. You feed them, they get your milk on their whiskers, they're back on your porch the next day meowing for more."

Jack and I hooked up at a neighborhood diner. He reminded me that lunch was on me. I dug into a double cheeseburger. Jack had a spinach salad (regular lettuce isn't good enough for him) with tomatoes, carrots, and all sorts of healthy stuff from other countries. On the side, he had a cup of soup that would've made a goldfish feel at home.

"Jack," I said, "what if you live to be one-hundred, but run out of money when you're ninety?"

"I'll be an old guy out looking for work," said Jack.

Jack went big brother on me, telling me how I needed to take better care of myself, that one day if I woke up in the state asylum wearing a diaper with doodle running down my leg he couldn't help me.

Most of the time Jack made sense, like he did now, but he and I'd had this pep-talk a couple of million times, so I tuned him out with a little daydream that starred Connie Sikma laying up on a pool table.

"Have you heard a word I said?" he asked.

"No, Jack, I'm sorry. It was crossing my mind why some guys shoot pool."

7

STEP ONE

I was "step one" in a lawsuit that had a bank from Omaha foreclosing on the manufactured home of Lucien Treadwell, a white boy who lived out in the country.

Manufactured-housing lawsuits are tough. The people who get thrown out of their homes have no place to go; they've got no place to eat; they've got no place to sleep, except maybe under the bridge, or the Salvation Army.

I call myself "step one" because I'm where the reality begins. You see, I show up at their door, they know the end is near. They know all those collection letters that were put in a pile, were never answered, would hopefully be part of a bad dream, aren't going away. Only thing going away is them.

And if a man thinks it's you throwing him out of his castle, he doesn't like you in the most personal sort of way. If things get bad, best thing you can do is keep it "all business." A man comes out of the house, calls you a filthy sumbitch, you make sure you keep it "all business." Or that man puts his dogs on you, they come running, their teeth wet and sharp, you don't show those dogs any fear, you keep it "all business."

You see, you're not just putting paper on that man, letting him know he's being sued. You're sniffing around his house, his home, what's precious and private to him. Because what makes the manufactured-house, lawsuit-paper process extra difficult is that before you drop your paper on some poor bastard you've got to find the serial number of that manufactured house, which usually sits on a seal on the side of the house with trees and bushes and boards around it because those people might be poor, but they're not stupid.

And when you've got that serial number for which there is no alternative way to do things, you make sure that serial number is the same, exact, identical number on the paper you've got to serve. That way there can be no doubt you've got the right man, you've got the right house, you've got everything right so far, you being "step one" in the manufactured-house, lawsuit-paper process.

To make my point, consider the last days of Casey Blaylock, a fellow private eye, who did the same manufactured-housing, lawsuit-paper work I do. Tough as a boot, he would fight you at the communion rail if you wanted it bad enough. Casey got hit in the back of the head with a two-by-four piece of wood, which, I add for detail, carried within it one large and sharp nail and which nail found its way to the center of Casey's brain in such a way as to put Casey's wife, whose name at this minute isn't coming to me, into the very bad position of leaving Casey, who by then was classified as dead by virtue of a straight line on a black screen, sucking on a tube for God knows how long or being left alone and unplugged to pass free and clear into the light.

Besides Treadwell's paper I had three other easy ones, none of them manufactured-housing lawsuits. Typically, I like to get people early, before they go to work, if they still have work. If I have to get several done the same day, I get the easy ones out the way first. I also plan my route the best I can to cut down on wasted driving.

I got up at 5:00, skipped breakfast, and did most of my driving in the dark. I had the three "easies" served before they were done with their Fruit 'N Fiber.

I hit Treadwell's place about ten in the morning. It was nicer than I thought. People will surprise you. You think some guy who lives in a manufactured home and isn't paying his bills is a deadbeat. And sometimes that's true. I've served bikers with tattoos who lived in manufactured homes that didn't have running water. Maybe there was a well out back. The place housed the biker, his girlfriend, the girlfriend's daughter, the girlfriend's daughter's boyfriend, all of them shacked-up along with their bikes and some old cars piled in the front yard.

But Treadwell had a cute, little picket fence that separated his yard from the acre or so of land the house looked to be parked on. It was skirted so you couldn't see the wheels, had a wooden deck for outdoor cooking, and a couple of tiny, neat flowerbeds scattered in the lawn that told me there was a woman who was going to lose her home too. The petition I was about to serve didn't name anybody but him, so I didn't figure him for married, but somebody made the premises look good and I didn't see it being a guy.

First thing I did was check for a dog. I stopped at the gate and shook my car keys. I didn't see a dog house, or dog shit in the yard, or a water bowl, and since no dog came running, I went in.

I learned my lesson about dogs the hard way. I once had a little wiener dog sneak up behind me and lock onto the heel of my boot. He didn't penetrate the boot, but I served the owner with his best friend hanging on my foot. The owner and I laughed so it wasn't all bad.

Now I carry dog biscuits and a can of mace. If I can't bribe him with the treats, I'll spray him if he looks like he's coming in for a bite. I'll spray him on the nose and on his tail if I can get a good shot. I wouldn't want somebody spraying pepper-juice up my ass.

I went directly to the seal that sits on the right side of the building as you face the door. The seal is in the same place at all times since the houses are mass produced. I copied down the serial number then read it very carefully against the number in my petition. I had the right house. To me, that's the toughest part since I'm always worried somebody might think I'm a burglar and blow my head off.

A human being about to get served is always a wildcard. Some people get a resigned look on their face, some people get surprised. It's a mixed bag of feelings only a student of human nature (such as me) can fully grip.

Normally, I'll get a picture of the party-to-be-served from the paralegal which, as you can visualize, is a good idea. But sometimes you don't have that luxury and you've got to go in blind with reliance on your ability to figure things out. I had no picture of Treadwell.

I knocked nice and polite to keep things calm inside the house. I sensed I was being watched through a window-blind which is no great surprise in this business. I knocked gentle again and heard footsteps heavy and thunderous coming toward the door.

"He ain't here."

A young, burly guy, who looked like he could be a construction worker, answered the door. He was clearly pissed off royal. I didn't know if he was Treadwell or not.

"I'm here to serve him in a lawsuit," I said.

"Treadwell ain't here," he said.

"He coming back soon?" I asked.

I figured if Treadwell was in the house he was watching me as we spoke or could hear the conversation from a place away from my line of vision.

"I don't know."

"Here," I said. I scribbled my phone number on the back of my business card then handed it to him.

"Can you read what I wrote on the back?"

"Why? You think I'm fucking illiterate?"

"No," I said. "My handwriting isn't always easy to read."

He took the card then shut the door. Maybe he was Treadwell. Maybe he was a roommate or family member who knew Treadwell was on the way to losing his home, which meant his life was getting ready to change too.

I went home, mowed the lawn, and then took it easy. I live in a modest, brick house located in a spot that gives me decent access to greater Houston, the coast, San Antonio, Austin, and most of central Texas. Once upon a time I lived in a manufactured-home. I liked it, was proud of it because it was mine. You want to break a man down, take something away from him he worked hard to get.

Next morning, I was back at it again; up early, a glass of juice, then the road. I hit Treadwell's with the same result. I knocked polite, heard footsteps, had the same guy answer the door in the same belligerent attitude.

"And you gave him the card?" I asked.

"I put it on the bar," he said.

He looked sideways at me, had his head cocked in a way that told me he wanted violence. I've been in my share of fights, read a lot of body language in my day. Body language says a lot about a man. A man wants to fight, he gets a look in his eye that's hard to mistake.

I nodded, knowing my trip out there was going nowhere, which left me thinking I'd make one more attempt at service and if it didn't result in me placing my paper into the hands of Lucien Treadwell, I'd "106" him. See, I'm not obliged to chase somebody the rest of my life, or from here to eternity. If I make three serious attempts that prove fruitless, I draw my affidavit that swears I made those attempts and when I made them. The court with jurisdiction over said matter issues an order that says I can substitute putting my paper directly in the hands of Mr. Treadwell with placing the paper in a place where he is sure to see it. For me, that's on the front door taped tight and secure so it won't blow away.

I must admit that Treadwell's door-buddy got me scared. I don't like being intimidated by anybody so it made me think I might be slipping in the way I carry myself. Once upon a time, if he came at me, I'd hit him ten times before he knew what happened. I'd split his face open like a ripe tomato.

The rest of the day, I went back to my workout routine. I'd let myself go for the last few months due to my own laziness. I followed ten minutes of jump-rope with push-ups then stomach crunches and thirty minutes on a body bag in the garage. At my peak, I was throwing about fifty punches a minute. I had a long way to go before I got back to that standard and I knew if I got into it at Treadwell's I was in no shape for combat. But for future situations, I wanted my body in fighting-shape.

That night I slept pretty good, no doubt from the exercise. Those endorphins the exercise nuts talk about are the real thing. And I was sharp as a knife when it came to thinking. All that fresh-oxygen blood in my brain had me two or three thoughts ahead of what was normal for me.

I was good to myself on the third trip out to Treadwell's in that I put my card in the door, my phone number once again on the back of the card, all neat and pretty and readable, then knocked but didn't wait for the door to open. Instead, I went back to my car where I waited for something to happen. When I got no action, I decided it was time for that affidavit.

I went home and, that afternoon, did my drafting. I got a form that sits in my computer with a handful of other legal documents Jack drew up for me. I get a case like this, I type in the particulars and I'm ready to go.

I had Sandy notarize my signature then I overnight-mailed the affidavit to the law firm handling the suit. Two days later I had my court-order directing me to hand the lawsuit paper to anyone at Treadwell's who was over eighteen, or, alternate to that, place it in a visible place.

Let me say something here about preparation. Preparation is the yeast that makes the cake rise. Some people might think a private eye out there serving lawsuit paper is a crazy cowboy running helter-skelter. Not true. The good ones, like me, got it down to a routine that makes us highly professional.

That night I sealed the court-order and the petition in a clear plastic envelope. I pealed off six good pieces of electrician's tape, one for each corner and one each for the top and bottom in the middle of the envelope. That way, I could walk up on Treadwell's door, tape the entire package to the door, and be out of there in a few seconds. You don't want to be fumbling around with plastic and tape at somebody's front door. And when you do your follow-up affidavit that says what you did, you want the court blessing your work. Because the Lucien Treadwells of this world, desperate as they are guaranteed to be, will say they never got served notice of the lawsuit which those of you, who have spent any time at all reading our Constitution, will know that if you don't give notice of the lawsuit you have fucked up due process.

I drove up to Lucien Treadwell's house for the fourth, and last, time. There was a guy in the front yard with his back to me. From his build, I could tell it was somebody different from the guy doing the door-answering. I noticed that the lawn chairs were all gone from the front yard and the flowers that looked so pretty two weeks ago were drying out.

"Lucien Treadwell?" I asked.

"Yeah? Who are you?"

I handed him the plastic envelope, tape and all.

"There's a lawsuit in there. You've been served."

He looked as beat as a guy can get. Made me feel lousy for all the poor suckers in the world who got up each morning thinking they had a chance.

"I don't care anymore," he said. "Come and take it."

I got home and called the paralegal handling the lawsuit. She asked me if I wanted to keep the manufactured-home, lawsuit-paper coming. She added I was the best paper-man she'd worked with. I liked hearing that so I told her I was her guy.

Couple of weeks later I was serving paper in the same part of the county where Treadwell's ex-house sat. I was backed up at a traffic light, wanting to go left, when I saw a guy who looked like the angry guy who met me at Treadwell's door. He was holding a sign that said he'd work for food. He could be real or he could be a panhandler, but either way he was a guy, standing alone in the heat, who needed money.

The traffic moved then stopped, leaving me alone at the light face-to-face with him, me not knowing for sure if it was the guy who answered Treadwell's door. (The two times we met, his face was twisted-up mean and he was behind glass.) But the way he looked at me led me to believe he was thinking the same thing.

Being raised on guilt, and holding myself directly responsible for him (whoever the hell he was) begging on that corner, I gave him a matching set of Jacksons. A guy in his predicament usually gets holy, thanks you from the bottom of his heart, blesses you, and guarantees you a place at the Lord's table. This guy took the money like it was the least I could do for him.

8

A GOOD NIGHT TURNS BAD

I left the *Bayou Bar & Grill* about eleven o'clock in the evening feeling like I'd had a pretty good night. I'd bill its owner for a pair of bartender audits and a review of the wait staff, all of which went smoothly. Taking into account my cash outlay for drinks and a meal, tips included, I figured to net about $150. Not bad for a night's work.

The *Bayou* is a large, redneck, honkey-tonk owned by Tim Fry. Tim owns three bar-restaurants. I've never met Tim. If that sounds crazy, it is. Our whole history is over the phone. The first time I tried to get his business (that being a cold-call over the phone) he wouldn't give me the time of day. But I wouldn't take "no" for an answer. I had nothing to lose by making another run at Tim. I sent him an envelope containing my cover-letter and a blank copy of my bartender and restaurant reports. I dare anyone in the mystery-shop business to top my written reports.

A week later he called me, impressed with my work. From that point forward I have visited his restaurants on a quarterly basis. I've been doing that for twenty years. I wouldn't know him if he came up to me and I'm sure he wouldn't know me if I did the same to him. I like the way he and I have done business all these years. I do the work, I mail him my reports, he sends me a check. And, I'm getting comfortable with email. I'm catching up with the twenty-first century.

I walked out onto the parking lot, an asphalt area about the size of a football field. On weekends the parking lot holds several hundred cars. I have to hand it to Tim, the

Bayou has it all: two huge bars, great food, (steaks, chicken, fish) live music, (country-western with occasional crossover) and a mammoth dance floor. I love doing mystery shops at the *Bayou*. I have a great time and, because the food and drinks are so affordable, I come away making good money. When the business is coming in, I wouldn't trade mystery shopping for any other line of work.

I jumped in my Toyota wanting to beat the rush of cars that would be filing out of the parking lot in the next hour or so. I hoped to get home and into bed before too late. I turned the key to the ignition and nothing happened. I turned it again with the same result. The battery was dead. I should have known better. The Toyota was a used pick-up that had been running like a top, but when I bought it I didn't think about the age of the battery.

I got out of my vehicle and headed back toward the restaurant. I was parked about one hundred feet away from the entrance, next to a Ford 150 pickup. I hadn't covered ten steps when the owner of the pickup, a tall, thin cowboy wearing boots and a Stetson hat, strolled up on me. I introduced myself, told him my problem, and like the good fellow he was, he pulled a pair of jumper-cables and had me going in no time. I followed him out of the lot, waiving to him as he went left and I went right.

I drove several blocks along the feeder road of IH 45 ready to jump on the freeway at the next onramp. It was July, a typical Houston night, hot and steamy. I had my air conditioner blasting me with cold air and the radio turned up too loud. With the windows up, what was the harm?

Between me and the onramp was one traffic light. I stopped at it with no one around me. Above and ahead of me cars hurried along IH 45 and to my immediate right, one lane over (I was in the left lane that would lead to the onramp) was an abandoned grocery store parking lot. As the Toyota idled at the light, it died.

I tried several times to start the truck with no luck. There was no one to call for help. I got out of the Toyota and pushed it across the lane to my right onto the grocery parking lot where I slid it into a parking space. It was midnight.

My brother Jack is big on AAA. He has, on a few occasions like birthdays and Christmas, given me and Sandy memberships. Jack preaches preparation. With roadside service, you're never stuck.

I didn't have AAA or any other roadside service. I'd let my membership expire, and Jack hadn't played Santa Claus last December. The *Bayou Bar & Grill* was in far north Houston, at least thirty miles from home. I knew Sandy was asleep. I didn't want to wake her up with a phone call. I didn't have enough cash on me for a cab, (I use my credit card when I go undercover) and I had no idea where or when the busses in that area ran. I locked my car nice and tight, walked to the onramp, and put out my thumb. I hadn't hitchhiked in a while.

A little history here: When Jack and I were boys, we hitchhiked everywhere. We hitchhiked to the Houston Astrodome for baseball games. We hitchhiked home from high school. When I was nineteen, a buddy and I hitched from Houston to Santa Monica California, all of it along Interstate 10. We didn't tell our parents how we got around.

I waited a few minutes as cars raced by. I've seen IH 45, or the other Houston freeways for that matter, bumper to bumper at two in the morning. IH 45 was busy, but moving along freely.

Before long, a car pulled over on the shoulder of the freeway not far up the onramp. I trotted up to a yellow Chevy Impala that coughed out steady clouds of exhaust.

The passenger, a young white guy, rolled down the window.

"Where to?" he asked.

"South Houston," I said.

He motioned me into the car with his right hand. He leaned forward pulling his bucket seat with him. I jumped in and settled into the back seat. The car was thick with marijuana. When I was young my pals and I smoked pot. It was fun and rebellious. Some of those guys are dead. I miss them all.

The driver was a black girl. I figured her for eighteen or nineteen years old. Her boyfriend (I made him for her boyfriend) looked about the same age. Neither one of them looked back, turned their heads, or said a word. She kept her hands glued to the steering wheel, he kept his attention straight ahead. I thought nothing of their behavior. It wasn't the first time the driver of a ride I'd hitched had nothing to say.

The Impala merged onto the freeway and sped south. I kept an eye on the speedometer. The driver kept her speed at fifty-five miles per hour which was five miles under the limit. A pair of stoners not wanting to attract the police, their caution made sense. I was pretty sure they'd hit me up for dope money and giving them a few bucks was the least I could do.

I took inventory of where I stood. I'd get home, shower, then hit the hay. Tomorrow morning I'd have Sandy drive me in her car to buy a new battery. She'd take me and the battery to my car where I'd get it started. I'd buy her lunch at a nice little Mexican cafe I knew of in the area. Then we'd both head home.

The Impala took an offramp well shy of my stop. I couldn't tell if I hadn't been clear about my drop-off point, or if they were getting tired of me. That made no sense, unless they were looking for conversation when they picked me up and my silence had put them off or had them thinking I was a bad man planning my next move. The quiet in the car was uncomfortable.

The exit ramp rolled into a dark feeder street. Best case scenario, I'd walk the remaining five miles and get home around three. I wouldn't get the sleep I wanted, but it was what it was.

I anticipated the Impala coming to a stop, me getting out and giving them ten bucks. They hadn't exactly given me curb service. Ten bucks was plenty for what little they had done for me.

The Impala took a quick right onto an asphalt road that ended several hundred feet behind a metal storage facility. It didn't stop until it was at the back of the building, out of sight from the freeway. There were high weeds around the perimeter of the building with nothing but a dim, yellow halo cast by a small light fixture attached to a tree swaying in the night breeze. I got the impression the two of them knew the area.

The white boy got out of the car. He pulled back the bucket seat. He motioned me out of the car. I did as he wanted. I knew what was happening. I wasn't born yesterday.

"Ever seen one of these?" he asked. He had a compact-looking pistol pointed at my face, not twelve inches from my nose.

"Too many times," I said.

I didn't figure he'd shoot me. But he was young, and those are the guys who sometimes shoot first and think later.

"Then you know what I want," he said.

I nodded and carefully took out my wallet. I handed him the twenty dollars I had on me.

"The cash is yours," I said, "but I need my driver's license." I hoped he wouldn't look in my wallet. In addition to my driver's license, my credit card and private investigator identification were there. I didn't need a kid with authority issues mistaking me for a cop.

"This all of it?" he asked.

"If there was more," I answered, "I'd be in a cab and not out here."

He snorted out some disapproval then tossed my wallet into the dark. I heard it hit somewhere on the asphalt outside the range of the yard light. Thank goodness it didn't land in those weeds.

He jumped into the Impala. The car took off. I stepped toward where I thought my wallet hit. I found it in a few minutes. I walked home and slept fully clothed on the couch. The next morning, I told Sandy, over coffee and French toast, about my evening. As planned, we got the battery and installed it into my car. We followed that with lunch at the Mexican cafe. I wasn't going to let some gooey little punk wreck a good night at the *Bayou Bar & Grill.*

9

ROOKIE MISTAKES

I watch people. I watch them for a living. People pay me to find out what's going on with those they loved and trusted once. Somebody's hubby or wife gets a little bored, they stray from the marital nest, and then guys in my profession get work. Stir in kids or money and the business of watching can be very good.

A lot of people, including the ones I do the watching for, take a dim view of my profession. I don't apologize for the work I chose. I'm good at it. It fits me like a glove. People knew how to act, how to treat each other with respect, I'd go hungry. But I won't go out of business. Human nature being the mess it is, I've got plenty of job security.

I turned private eye twenty years ago. Before that I bartended, something I did long enough to hate. I hated getting out of bed, I hated going to work, I hated my life. And everybody knows what happens when you hate. You get into patterns. Bad patterns. Unhealthy, unhappy, unholy patterns.

I got my first job under license from an accountant by the name of Paul Black. Life of me, I can't remember how he got my name. Maybe my brother Jack put him on to me.

I met with him in his office, the kind of place you'd expect from a bean counter. He had a big desk, a lot of paper on it, in a building full of guys dressed just like him. He was a wide, soft-looking guy who took notes and asked a lot of questions. Being new to the trade, I barely knew shit from shinola. But I didn't tell Black. Far as he was concerned, I was Humphrey Bogart.

"Lovely, isn't she?" asked Black. He handed me a picture of his ex-wife, a tall, athletic girl who'd fit real nice into any guy's trophy case. She looked at least ten years younger than Black which told me he had money. Joe Schmo doesn't get a woman like that unless he's got some coin.

"Yes, very," I said.

He gave me another picture, one of his son, a kid who looked about twelve with blond, curly hair sticking out from a ball cap and holding onto a glove.

"Pamela pushed him into sports. I preferred that Charles focus on his studies but his mother comes from a family of athletes. You know, people who think that grunting and sweating and putting points up on a scoreboard is some sort of religious experience. He has no future in sports. He doesn't even like athletics. Why would you push your child into something he doesn't like?"

He went into the reason he called me. The ex, he was sure, was leaving the kid home alone at night while she shacked up. Who was nailing her wasn't his business but he wanted custody of the kid, and mamma's basic instincts gave him an opening.

"Why don't you just ask your son?" I asked.

"I don't want him caught up in this," said Black.

"Who's he want to live with?" I asked.

"Does that really figure into your work, Mr. Spivey?"

I took Mr. Black's little scolding like a man then proceeded to tell him how August Spivey did business. This was twenty years ago, long enough for little girls bouncing on their daddy's knee to become Dallas Cowboy cheerleaders. At the time, I didn't have a written contract. It wasn't until later when Jack educated me on the beauty of the written word that I gave in and, with his help, wrote what I meant and meant what I wrote.

"Mr. Spivey, but what happens if this deal between us goes awry?"

"You mean what happens if I screw you?"

"Well, yes."

I stuck out my hand for demonstration, reserving the deal-closing for later.

"You see this right here?" I asked.

"Yes, I do."

"If that's not good enough, I can leave right now. For what it's worth, I've got no doubts about you."

So, the accountant and I did grown-up business. I told him I required two hours up front. At seventy-five bucks an hour, it came to one-hundred-fifty bucks I needed to walk away with.

"To be clear," I said, "you want me to follow her home from work then sit down on her until midnight. She goes anywhere, I follow."

"That's right," said Black.

"Walk me through this," I said, "does it matter where she goes, as long as she goes?"

"I do want to substantiate that she's spending the entire night out. My lawyer tells me that is important. The character, the occupation, the habits of her lover might tip things in my favor should the other party be, shall we say, unsavory."

"OK," I said. "If she goes, I follow. How long you want me to stay with her if she stays over somewhere?"

"Until she leaves. Pamela is highly structured. She gets up religiously at five, does her yoga, eats, showers, goes to work. My guess is she won't leave there a minute after four in the morning if not sooner. She'll want to be home by five."

We shook hands. It was a little clumsy, like we'd been saving ourselves for that special moment. He wrote me a check, a photocopy of which I have to this day. It being Monday after four o'clock, he and I agreed that Tuesday was prom night.

I went home, thought out my plan for the next day. That night I made friends with a lot of sheep. Next morning, I was up drinking black coffee like it was the last thing between me and a future that didn't hold much promise.

At the time, I lived in a small apartment in a house the other half of which was rented to a young skinhead who went by the name of Chris. I can't remember if Chris had a last name or if he had one and I didn't want to know. Chris was tattooed up his right arm but didn't have a mark on his left. He told me his body was a canvas, him being choosey about the next artist who put a needle to him.

Chris liked white people like most of us humans like the act of breathing. I'm white, so he treated me friendly. First night in my place I thought I had a rattlesnake under my bed. Try sleeping with that. Turns out Chris had a pair of rattlers in a cage he kept in his room the other side of the wall from where my head touched the pillow. Most nights I heard rattlers.

At quarter to four on Tuesday I pulled in the parking lot of a tall building that made me think of a stack of poker chips. Black's former wife didn't have to work. The divorce left him with his profession and his balls but not much more. But she went back to work as a paralegal, the job she did before she married him. My guess is she got bored with a big house, a small kid, and a life full of empty. He gave me the make of her car, a black Nissan *SUV*, and the door she came out of regularly. I spotted her car, parked in the next row over, my truck pointed so I could jump on her quick.

At a couple of minutes after four, she came out. She looked good on Kodak, better in person, the kind of ass and legs that show up on a health-club junkie. She pulled out into traffic. I was in her pocket like a penny in a pair of tight jeans.

A couple of thoughts on tailing somebody from a guy who's been at it a while. It's hard, but sitting and waiting is harder. You sit in a parking lot, maybe some citizen sees you, takes his role serious, gets the impression you're a rapist on the prowl or some other form of bad-guy out shopping for opportunity, it can go bad. Nothing is tougher for me than sitting in a school parking lot with a bunch of little kids running around. You get the picture.

At 4:30, the ex and the kid came out of a high-end elementary school in a high-end part of town. I followed them to a house a few minutes from the school. I parked down the street with a good view of the front door and the driveway. If she left unnoticed, she'd have to go through the backyard and climb a fence.

Nowadays, a private investigator parks on a street, say in a subdivision, he has to report to the cops or the security people he's going to be there a while. That way, they don't come rolling up to his car and make a scene with him. Back then, there was no set of rules like that. You were on your own. They pulled up on you, you better have your license, you better be polite, you better hope they weren't having a bad day.

I sat down on her until midnight. She didn't leave the house. No car came out of the driveway. If being at home with your kid makes you a good parent, then she was a good parent, at least for that night.

Next morning around ten I called Black at his office.

"She was a good girl," I said, wishing I'd been more respectful.

"She didn't leave?" asked Black.

"No, and I was on her like glue from the minute she left work, picking up your son, then going home. It will be in my report."

"I just know she's up to something. Follow her again tonight."

"Same time, same place?" I asked.

"Yes," said Black, "do it again."

I cleaned up my notes, ate a bowl of chili for lunch, then took a nap. I woke up at 3:00. I stepped in the shower, getting just wet enough that I wouldn't smell badly in case I mingled with my fellow man. At three thirty, I drove back to her office. She came out at four and I was on her again. She picked up her son at school and took him home. I parked down the street with the same view of her house, but back a couple of hundred feet from where I parked the night before. At 6:00, her Nissan pulled out of the driveway. With her SUV having tinted windows, I couldn't tell who was in the car. It could've been anybody, her, her and the kid, who knew?

I followed her through drive-time traffic, zig-zagging in and out of cars, to a quiet street about thirty minutes away. She pulled into the driveway of a wood frame house that would've been a castle to me, but not a woman like her. I went down the street where I made a quick turn-around in a driveway then drove by as I saw the door open and her go in. I did a pretty smart thing, something that should come natural to a private investigator, by that I mean I got the plates on the other car in the driveway. I saw enough of her going in the front door to know it was the former Mrs. Black. She went in solo. There was nobody with her, the kid included.

The street dead-ended into a railroad tie, behind that, trees and high weeds. The only way out for a car was back down the street the way we came in. I did one more turnaround, at the open end of the street where it connected with the feeder road of the freeway. Facing the house, the far end of the street plugged up, I knew there was no way she could leave without me seeing her.

I settled in for the evening at 6:45. First thing I did was write down the plates of the other car. To this day my alternate office is the car I'm driving. I keep two pens, a notepad, extra business cards, a map, and a couple of dollars in quarters inside a tidy pouch that clips nicely to my visor. At my house, I've got a real office with a desk and a phone and a computer, but it's my car or truck where I feel at home and do my life's best work.

I opened a thermos of coffee and read for a while from a baseball book about Willie Mays that had my recent attention. I read until dark, which came about nine, it being daylight savings. I put the book down on the seat next to me. I had my driver's license, vehicle registration, and investigator's license handy just in case one of those lawmen I talked about earlier came by. None did.

Then I waited. Oh, how I waited! It being a quiet street, not much went on. A couple of cars came dragging in around eight or so but by dark everybody was tucked in for dinner and family living.

The coffee kept me going along with a rich and vivid imagination about me in front of a urinal the first chance I got. At three thirty in the morning, I saw Pamela Black's SUV back out of the driveway. I leaned away from the window, into the passenger side of the car as she went by.

Next morning at ten o'clock, I dropped by the DMV where I ran the plates. The DMV was close by, a vehicle search was cheap, so I went ahead with it unauthorized thinking that if Black didn't want it, I'd eat the cost.

The car was listed in the name of one Jayne Miller. I made a simple search through the phone book where I found the name at an address on the street I spent the night on. I called Black early afternoon.

"I don't know anybody by that name," he said. "Did you get a look at her?"

"No," I said, "she went in, didn't come out until three-thirty. I caught a quick look when the door opened, but I couldn't see who answered it."

"What should I do?" he asked.

"Look, it's Thursday. Let me drive by this weekend. I'll do it for free. Maybe I'll get a visual of this woman."

I filled in my notes and rested up the next day and a half. There was one driveway that served the house Chris, his rattlers and I shared. The entrance to my place had a nice little awning over the front door that made for a good place to grill. I threw a steak on along with a half chicken and spent Thursday afternoon with my feet up.

Saturday, I did my drive-by. It being April, I figured to catch Miller out in the yard any time in the afternoon. I drove by around four o'clock and got lucky.

"The woman," said Black, "can you describe her?"

"I'd say thirty, maybe thirty-five. Short hair. Dirty blond. I'm guessing medium height, slight build."

"And you say she and Pamela were affectionate?"

"Yeah. They were sitting in the front yard in lawn chairs."

"How affectionate?"

"Well, hands were held. I saw a kiss."

"You're sure."

"Yeah, I'm sure."

I recommended that I sit down at least one more night on the house. Black agreed. The following Tuesday I was back at it again. By now, I knew the drill: work, school, night time at Miller's house, then back home around between three and four in the morning. Pamela didn't disappoint.

I finished my report, a detailed summary of times, places, people. I included a photocopy of the DMV report and delivered my package to Black in his office. He came across to me as the kind of guy who could simmer for a long time and then one day blow up. The look on his face told me Pamela's romp, helpful or not to his case, put a crack in his china-plate world.

A couple of days later I got a call from his lawyer, a sandy-voiced woman who wasn't happy with me.

"You didn't get pictures?" she asked.

"No."

"Why not?"

"Black didn't ask for them," I said.

"But, doesn't it go without saying that you get pictures?"

"I can still get pictures," I said.

"No, it's too late. We filed suit. The cat's out of the bag."

She asked me if I was available to testify at the hearing, me being the only evidence Black had. I showed up nervous in a new shirt, new jeans, polished boots and the only jacket I owned. Once I hit the stand, vessel of truth that I was, my nerves took a turn for the better.

The kid wasn't in the room; neither was the girlfriend. Pamela Black figured out early it was her word against mine. It didn't go good.

I counted up my hours and sent my final bill to Black. I didn't charge him for the DMV search, the Saturday drive-by, or the testimony in court. All of that, I figured, was on me.

I waited like a Greek statue for my check, an amount that came in at $2250 when you figure thirty net hours of work at $75 an hour. I called Black a few times, got his secretary, not him.

I knew I made two big mistakes. The first one was not shooting the pictures. Now, I'd shoot the former Mrs. Black and Jayne Miller with a cell-phone camera or one of a bunch of cameras you can buy at any security store. And back then a simple Kodak would've sealed the deal.

Other mistake I made was not getting the deal in writing. I deliver civil process, or do a small job, I still don't force the contract. It's not worth it, and most people won't sign it anyway. It's a big job, five hundred bucks or more, we celebrate over paper.

Sixty days went by. I was on to another job. I was out on the driveway one day, my puss sour as a lemon over the Black deal, when Chris walked up. You see, I had it in mind to use the Black money for an apartment in a rattler-free zone.

"I think you're going about this the wrong way," he said, once I went story-teller on him.

I figured his answer to my dilemma would involve some rough stuff, maybe a rattle snake in a box.

"Write him a letter," said Chris. "Appeal to his sense of fairness. You'd be surprised how some people react when they are confronted with honor."

I sent Black a hand-written letter where I told him I was a guy making an honest living. I reminded him I put in thirty sleepless hours on a street where nobody knew me. I requested that he pay me half of what he owed me. At the end, I said, "Mr. Black, it's time you did the right thing."

Two weeks later I got a check for the full amount. As a little reward, I took Chris to my favorite eatery, a barbecue joint called Smokey's. Smokey's is gone now, and I miss it like a good Catholic misses communion. You like chicken, ribs, or pork, slathered up in grease, Smokey's was fine-dining.

Smokey, the owner, was as nice as your gramps and dark as a moonless midnight. God bless him, he died one evening in the kitchen cooking, which is what he loved and kept his heart pumping for a bunch of years.

I didn't think about race until Chris and I took a table. I was worried as hell he might lean over and say, "I don't eat the black man's food," or something just as bad. But after some ribs, and beans, and cold beer, the black-white thing never came up. Go figure!

10

LIFE I CHOSE

I'm no zen guy. I don't go around thinking that if you're patient good things happen when they should. If you want your life to go good, you gotta have a plan and you gotta execute that plan. Otherwise, you're just another day-dreamer walking around with his thumb up his ass.

I was bartending in Phoenix, Arizona. I moved out there thinking maybe sunshine and pretty women would give me the jump start I needed. Six nights a week I poured Jack Daniels. My day off, I drank him.

My drinking buddies were a retired judge, an ex-boxer, and a guy I'm pretty sure was a thief.

The boxer was a washed-up middleweight not smart enough to call dumb. But he had enough left in him to smack the shit out of me so I treated him respectfully.

The thief, I never let get close. A waitress where I worked had a special thing going with him once upon a time, a secret thing, (he was married, you get the picture), and she told me confidentially how he made his living.

The judge looked like the softest one in the bunch. He was short, round as a berry, the kind you could push around easily. But the way the other two treated him, never interrupting him, always listening to what he had to say, made it clear he was their alpha-dog. Power is a funny thing.

I first met the three of them where I worked. They sat at the bar, serious drinkers who put alcohol ahead of women. The judge did most of the talking. After a year or so of them coming in periodically, never more than once or twice every three months, we started drinking together at Katy's, a dark, little, Irish dive six blocks from the bar where Mr. Daniels and I did our life's work.

"Tell me about this business you're in," I said. We were at Katy's.

See, one way or another, I was getting out of bartending. I was getting too old for it. It was hard on my lungs, hard on my legs and hands, hard on my point of view. The only drunk I like being around is me.

"Well, it goes like this," said the judge. He then went on to tell me about the mystery-shop business, a business you, or somebody you pay, goes, sits down in a bar, up close and personal with the bartender, and watches that bartender to see if he or she steals. You get in good with a bar owner, maybe he owns a chain of bars, you can make pretty good money in such a business.

"So, you could watch me someday," I said.

"You been watched already," said the judge, then he and the boxer and the thief had this quiet little laugh on me.

"And?" I asked.

"I'm happy to say you are a very honest man."

So, right there, across from the alpha-dog judge, his goofy boxing pal, and a thief, a plan formulated in the mind of August Spivey. All my life I've been helping other guys get rich. How about I spend my precious blood, sweat, and tears, not to mention time, making myself the beneficiary of my hard work?

That night I was so crazy-pumped I couldn't sleep. Sleep which, by the way, didn't come easy to me on a normal night. But if you threw the sweet and seductive smell of success into the mix, my head was full of little tornados telling me that if I didn't seize that opportunity I may as well accept bartending the rest of my life which, in case you haven't figured it out, made August Spivey a very unhappy man.

So now I had that plan and I had to execute that plan, right? I asked for one more sit-down visit at Katy's with the judge who I told up-front and immediately that my plan was to go back to Texas and do what he was doing.

"Long as you're not doing it around here, you know, competing with me," he said, and laughed, but I know humor when I hear it, and this thing that came out the judge's mouth had nothing funny about it.

He and I spent the afternoon together, his two pals there as usual, so close it looked like three heads, six arms, all in one body, him telling me the finer points of mystery-shopping, how I'd be a natural, me being a bartender for such a long time that I could spot anything unusual going on behind a bar.

"In Arizona," he said, "you got to have a private eye license."

"How hard is that?" I asked.

"Well, here, you got to pass a test, show the state you're a good boy, not a criminal, you know, so on and so forth."

Once upon a time August Spivey would look upon such a task as was described by the judge, (me dealing with the state, in my case the State of Texas), as a problem that ran contradictory to my inclination for flying under the radar at all times.

But this was a clear-cut case of how bad did I want things to get better, meaning I wanted more than the level of near-poverty and unbearable dissatisfaction my life had brought to the table so far.

I called my brother in Texas.

"Jack," I said, "it's Augie."

"Yeah, Augie, what's up?"

I shared a little story of personal redemption with my brother, me wandering in the desert of lost hope, my soul parched up so dry it wouldn't produce anything spiritual, until one day along came a judge and a pair of his buddies, (none of them out to benefit their fellow man), who, by accident, planted within me a seed that flowered into my own Garden of Eden.

"What the heck are you talking about, Augie?" asked Jack.

"There's something special going on here Jack and you can be part of it."

I settled down into a state of psychology and metaphor, then told Jack that I had this great idea to start a private eye business, me turning into a Texas billionaire someday, if not sooner.

"I insist on helping," said Jack, all sarcastic because Jack had his own story and because Jack had heard his share of wild dreams, me being the dreamer of those dreams, to the point he only believed in what he could touch or taste or see or smell, and *not* "sure-as-hell," false promises that came out of me like candy out of a gum-ball machine.

But I dismissed Jack's very clear lack of faith in me, pushing myself forward to the golden chalice that wouldn't let me take my eye off it, that kept calling me, that kept reminding me that if I gave up then, I would give up forever so I said, "Jack, I need this one bad."

Then Jack changed back into the brother I know and asked, "OK, Augie, what can I do?" and I said, "Jack, what's it take to be a private eye in Texas?"

"I don't know," said Jack, "off top of my head but give me a day or two and I'll find out."

You see, right then and there I knew I was on the way to things bigger and better and brighter and broader because, if I knew Jack, he'd get me what I needed. Jack's got this internal set of rules that says that if you tell someone you're going to come through for them, you've made a promise you've got to keep.

A couple of days later, me cooking up all sorts of favorable outcomes, (that life-change idea having me all wound-up), I got the call from Jack who told me Texas and Arizona may as well be the same state. This meant somebody like me who wanted into the observation business was required to have a private eye license, which meant I had to prove up my good character which for me was (I hoped) OK because I'd never done anything terribly wrong in the eyes of God or illegal when it came to Joe Citizenry.

But I was also required to work three years (minimal) under the good auspices of a real private eye so as to learn the profession in a manner that would allow me to know what I was doing before I went out and did it.

This unexpected item, compliments of the State of Texas, caused me to go sleepless over a period of time which resulted in a mindset I will call crabby. But in my new venture, in which I decided failure was a decision I would not allow myself to make, I took it upon myself to call that body of legal people that regulated such matters, said body being the Private Investigation Board for the State of Texas, which informed me in a polite, but definite way that the three-year experience thing did not, I repeat, did not, apply to a licensed attorney. This meant that any lawyer in the State of Texas could take the private eye test without three years working for somebody else, which also meant that said lawyer who avoided said three-year thing could also hire me and in doing so I would fulfill my own three-year thing, that is *if* said lawyer and I could make it work without us killing each other.

And who did I know who filled such a profile? I didn't tell Jack because I knew that if I called him and proposed that he become a private eye for the benefit of one August Spivey, I would get a swift and unmerciful "no!"

So, in my brain, I developed a special compartment that gave me clarity and focus in a way which allowed me to file my plan for Jack under "Things I Need To Do Later" and decided that when I approached the subject of me working for Jack in a capacity that had him, as the private eye, and me, as the private eye student, I would offer him a partnership in my "can't miss" venture.

And even Jack, who lives by rules and hates the thrill of life coming at him unexpectedly, couldn't turn down such a chance of a lifetime, could he?

Well, wouldn't you know the day I left Arizona I experienced a classic case of "cold feet." Was I doing the right thing? I'd sold all my material stuff, which included a television that cost that me some good coin, (my first TV, a color Sony, had been pawned by Blacky Upjohn, no longer a friend of mine), my bed, and clothes over and above what didn't fit in the bedroll that was strapped to the back of my Harley.

I said my goodbyes. You see, despite him having me "shopped" by the judge, I still had a soft spot in my heart for Terry Frank who hired me as a bartender in the first place. I've quit bartending jobs on a phone call, sometimes not even that much, but Terry was always equally straight-up with me, and, if you don't count the mystery-shop, in my desire to be a straight-up with him, and because I wished to keep a degree of rehirableness with Terry, I gave him two-weeks-notice, which, by the way, he appreciated and guaranteed that if I ever came back his way he'd hire me or point me to a job which was good because there were very few bars and bartenders in Phoenix who Terry didn't know.

I also said goodbye to Nicky Thomas. Nicky and I had a casual thing, a thing we both made clear was of a temporary nature, but you know how that goes. People get feelings mixed into things, it's never easy if they break up. So, after things got a little misty we both realized we had separate destinies written in a big book somewhere and we both needed to go on to the next chapter.

In Fort Stockton, I thought hard about what I'd left behind in Arizona. I could've made a phone call to Terry Frank and been pouring Jack Daniel's the next night. And I could have called Nicky with a promise that it was me and her together forever. I might have had that door reopen too.

But I kept on going. I got back to Texas. Jack took the test, he wasn't happy about it, but he hired me so I could fulfill my dream. Three years later I obtained my own license that allowed me to move legally and comfortably in the private eye business. And I'm good. No, I'm the best. I learned the hard way, the school of hard knocks. And when I say I'm the best, I'm not just the best of the rest, or the best of the best, but the best of the best of the best of the best at what I do.

Fast-forward twenty years. You do something long enough, the glim and the glam, the bling and the blang eventually wears off so you come to realize it's a job and sometimes it takes a kick in the pants to remind you that not many people get to live out their dream.

So years later, Jack and I got together at the funeral of Jimmy Brown. Jimmy was a pal from way back. He and I rode bikes, played ball, got in and out of trouble together. Jack wasn't as close to Jimmy as I was, but Jack's got this sentimental thing he insists is curiosity when it comes to the old neighborhood.

Jimmy had a nice funeral. At the end of the service he was postmarked for Heaven but even Jimmy would tell you it was no sure thing. I saw some of the old farts, who once upon a time were young bucks with me. You get old, all that hard crust and meanness that comes from growing up makes you wonder if you were pals with anybody. But every now and then somebody surprises you, maybe a spark of who they were comes out accidentally which brings that same spark out of you, and takes you back, helps you feel who you once were.

Out in the parking lot Jack and I took a minute. Funeral limos were going by, but I didn't go to the graveyard. I didn't want to see Jimmy get filed away. My day would come. Would it be so bad? You had a life well-lived, got some things done, and your time wasn't cut too short, maybe death was a satisfying thing.

"Jack, you ever wonder if you could do it over, you might choose something else?"

"No," said Jack. "I don't allow it. It can only make you unhappy."

I then did a little pissing and moaning about making bills and living month-to-month in a world of lousy people, which I knew immediately was a mistake that I wished I could take back because the listener of my complaint was a guy who held people accountable.

"Sorry, Augie," said Jack, "it's the life you chose."

11

AUGIE REFLECTS

Chuckie Mayes and I got together at his place to watch football. His girlfriend was out of town, and Sandy needed a break from me. The Cowboys were playing the Giants in New York.

Chuckie is a huge Dallas Cowboy fan. When they win, he's happy. When they lose, it puts him in a bad mood. I'm not a Cowboy fan, but I like pro football. My favorite team was the Houston Oilers. I grew up with them. They were mostly lousy, but I loved them. When they left town, it killed me. Things change, I know. Life will teach you that.

Chuckie is a fellow private investigator. He's about eighty-percent redneck. We get along fine. He and I help each other out. If one of us is swamped with work, the other picks up the slack and we split the fee. In that way, we have each other's back. We both know what it's like living month-to-month, worrying about when the next job is coming in. I've loaned him money; he's done the same for me. I wish the rest of the world was made of nothing but Chuckies.

It was half-time and the Cowboys were down by three. They had three turnovers that gave the Giants thirteen easy points. Chuckie was going nuts. He was pacing the room and yelling at the television. My brother Jack got the same way back when we watched the Oilers. I suggested to Chuckie that he and I go for beer. We'd finished off a six-pack of Miller High Life, the champagne of bottled beer, and I wanted some air. Chuckie's place is neat thanks to his girlfriend Candi, but, when she's out of town, it gets cluttered fast.

We jumped into his pickup and headed to the *Last Stop*, a convenience store that sits about a mile from Chuckie's manufactured home. The *Last Stop* is on a lonely corner out in the country where two asphalt county roads come together. I guess that's how it gets its name.

A big Asian guy runs the place. His name is Henri (pronounced *ONREE*) because, according to Chuckie, Henri is part French and part Viet Namese. When it comes to sports or politics, Henri thinks he knows a lot which gets under my skin.

We pulled into the parking lot. Another pickup was there. Otherwise, no one was around. I figured everyone was at home watching football or attending late-morning church.

Chuckie and I hopped out of his truck and walked past the other pickup. It was black but I didn't know the model. Auto vehicles have never been a source of curiosity for me.

Its owner was a skinny white-guy with a cowboy hat pulled down over his eyes. He wore a T-shirt, blue jeans, and had a tattoo of something I couldn't make out on his left arm. He was smoking a cigarette. I noticed all of this while he stood at the back end of the pickup with the tailgate down as Chuckie and I went by. Typically, I say, "hello" to people when they make eye-contact with me, but this guy didn't look up from the tool box he was sorting through.

We walked into the convenience store. I consider a stop for beer as necessary, not convenient. I've tried that line on people from time to time and get an occasional laugh. I noticed the small, color television that Henri kept on a table behind the counter was on the station that carried the Cowboys. It looked like half-time might be coming to an end so I figured we'd get our beer and beeline it back to Chuckie's.

I wasn't ten steps into the store when I felt cold mettle on the back of my neck. I was facing Henri and Chuckie was to my near right. Henri's eyes got big. So did Chuckie's. Nothing was making sense.

Then *everything* made sense. The skinny guy in the cowboy hat, wearing a red bandana over his face, came into view.

"You ah snake," snapped Henri. (I neglected to say earlier that Henri's English wasn't what I'd call the *American* variety.)

The gunman nodded to the register. Bear in mind that the gun was on *my* neck, not Henri's or Chuckie's.

"You motha is snake. You fatha is snake. You chilren will be snakes," continued Henri.

"Henri, open the fucking register and give him the money now," I said. Chuckie nodded in agreement. Both he and I had our hands up.

Henri reached into the register and pulled out the cash. I figured it for a few twenties and a couple of smaller bills. I'd say maybe thirty to fifty bucks changed hands.

"In there," said the gunman. He pointed down the food aisle with bread and cookies and snacks to the cooler at the back of the store.

Henri came from behind the counter and he, Chuckie, and I, with our hands up, marched toward the cooler, the gunman behind me with the pistol at my back. I was relieved that Henri didn't come from behind the register pumping lead. Chuckie told me once that Henri kept a sawed-off shotgun underneath the counter. There was no way I would escape lead if bullets started flying.

But I was *sweating* bullets.

"On the floor," commanded the gunman. His voice was muffled by the bandana and I sensed he was talking in an intentionally low voice. I hoped like hell the bandana didn't slip down exposing his face.

We got down on the floor, Henri farthest away, then Chuckie, then me. I was closest to the gunman, the open door to the cooler only three feet away. The floor was cold and damp from what I figured was a mopping Henri gave it that morning. What would happen if another customer walked into the store? Things could get out of control fast. Henri was still yelling insults at the robber. If I lived through this, I considered clobbering Henri's ass.

"Henri," I said, "shut the fuck up."

The gunman kicked me hard in my exposed ribs. I didn't see it coming. With my belly on the floor and my arms extended, there was nothing between my rib cage and his pointed boots but my skin.

"Hooooo!" I groaned. The kick momentarily knocked the wind out of me. I had enough left in me to quietly recite the Lord's prayer. If I was going over to the other side, I wanted my passport stamped.

"Any of you looks up, you're dead," said the gunman. "Keep your heads down for five minutes or you're dead. And if I get flushed back in here for any reason, you're dead." He kicked me again in the ribs. It hurt like hell, but I did best I could to stay quiet.

We didn't put a clock on it. I heard his truck speed off. The three of us honored the five-minute rule. It probably went longer than that but as you might guess, time has a funny way of speeding up or slowing down depending on your mental state.

From my position on the floor I saw Chuckie raise

98

his head. Had his head exploded from a gunshot it would not have surprised me. Henri raised his head, then I raised mine. Through the glass of the cooler I could see no one in the store. From the cooler door, it was clear the black pickup was gone. We walked single file back to the counter. The store, except for the television, was strangely quiet. You could have heard a pin drop; my senses were at their best because of the adrenaline that had rushed through me.

Henri called the police. A county sheriff rolled up in a few minutes. He took a description of the robber and his vehicle from the three of us. None of us arrived at the same description of the guy or, except for the color of the truck, were any help on the make of the pickup or its plates. The sheriff estimated the truck had been stolen the night before or early that morning. No sense in getting upset about the details.

Chuckie and I bought our beer and drove home. We came in to see the Cowboys miss a tying field goal with less than a minute to play. The Giants ran out the clock. Chuckie wasn't as unhappy with the outcome as he would have been normally.

"Chuckie," I asked, "you were quiet back there. Did you think we were gonna die?"

"Yeah," said Chuckie, " I thought it was my time."

"Were you ready for it?" I asked.

"What do you mean?" he asked.

"With your life," I said. "Laying there, on the floor, did you think you'd missed out on anything if that was the end?"

"No," he said, "when the universe calls, that's it. What about you, Augie?"

"I had a crazy thought. I figured some people die too young, some people live too long. Not many people die at the right time."

12

ANOTHER CLOSE CALL

I was twenty years a private investigator. Work was going good. Plenty of lawsuit paper was coming my way, my undercover jobs were picking up, and a suspicious hubby was paying me good money to keep an eye on his wandering, naughty spouse. Then I got sick, very sick, *graveyard* sick.

I felt a cold coming on the weekend before Labor Day. The symptoms we're the usual: sore throat, dripping nose, swollen sinuses. When I was a kid, colds came and went in no-time. I'd get it, blow my nose for a day or two, cough for an afternoon, and it was over. Not anymore, this rascal wouldn't go away.

The weather didn't help. September may as well have been July. The temperature never got below ninety, and was up near one hundred most of the month. I was driving a used red Toyota truck I bought from a pal after my Ford pickup had gone to truck heaven. A damn fine vehicle was that Toyota. It was ten years old and had one-hundred thou on it when I bought it. I drove the hell out of it and put another one hundred thousand plus miles on it. Unlike my Ford, the Toyota had air conditioning when I bought it, but the A/C had died and I hadn't gotten it fixed.

I dress for comfort. My usual outfit is a pair of blue jeans, a ball cap, and a Hawaiian shirt that feels like a million bucks on me. I must have fifteen of those shirts, compliments of my brother Jack who gives me one every

August on my birthday, the last one included. Driving around in that heat and humidity had those fancy birthday shirts soaked so bad I was dripping on the upholstery.

And I couldn't sleep. What else is new? I never rest. I come from a family of nighttime worriers. On a good night, I *might* get five hours of sleep; most nights its three to four. With work piling up on me, feeling overwhelmed, I was getting an hour or two of sleep at most. Some nights I didn't sleep any.

October came around. The weather cooled off a little. It was football season. (I like the pros. The college game isn't for me.) The cold lingered. I figured it more for an allergy. Some days were better than others. I carried around a mild fever with me that came and went but hit me hardest at night when I was resting in my easy chair. During the day, driving around, now that I wasn't sweating like a derby winner, I felt on the regular side. I'd serve a guy a lawsuit paper, or go undercover in a bar, the whole time dismissing my rundown feeling as a temporary event sure to clear up when the cedar settled down. But at night, my eyes burned and my body ached. Whatever had me wouldn't let go.

Then it hit me like a truck. It was Thanksgiving. Jack had dropped in for a piece of apple pie and brotherly advice which he gives out freely and more than I usually want. I kept breaking away from our conversation to step out into the back yard for air. I had tickets for Sandy and I to see a Dave Mason concert that was coming through town that weekend but I was so sick we gave the tickets away. By Friday night I was gasping for air; short, choppy breathes that felt like fish hooks ripping at my left lung.

I spent Saturday in my easy chair sitting upright. I couldn't lay down, I couldn't stand up, it hurt that bad. My breathing was still shallow. I could inhale only so much. I watched football nonstop but I couldn't tell you who was playing.

I broke down and called EMS thinking I was having a heart attack. Sandy was working at the prison, it was just me and our dog, Luther, at home. I stretched for the phone which sat outside my limited comfort zone. Those fish hooks in my left lung had gotten sharper and deeper. I struggled with talking. My voice was weak, it wheezed. I told the 911 operator the front door was unlocked and that the EMS people should walk in without me answering the door.

They arrived twenty minutes later. I whispered that my chest was killing me and that I could barely breathe. An EKG showed nothing was wrong with my heart. I was happy to hear that but I wasn't convinced that something wasn't killing me. They left.

Sandy came home and made me a plate of chicken fajitas, black beans, and guacamole. Normally I'd inhale a meal like that and come back for more. I had no appetite whatsoever. Sandy threw some aluminum foil on my plate and set it in the ice box.

I sat up that night in my chair while Sandy slept in our bedroom. I didn't sleep a wink. When I wasn't out of breath, I was worried about how much work I would miss. Luther curled up at the foot of my chair. He sleeps in bed with me and Sandy but he always stays close by me whenever I'm having problems. He's one hell of a dog.

The next morning Sandy offered to cook up some bacon and eggs for me. I wasn't interested. She left for work worried about me but I told her I'd be OK. By 10:00, I was in trouble. I thought I might be dying. I dialed up the prison number and reached Sandy on the phone.

"Sandy, I gotta have you right now. I'm in a bad way," I said.

She rushed home. It took me thirty minutes, with her help, to get dressed. I could barely walk to her car. Try walking bent over with no air getting into your lungs. She pulled into the local community hospital. Getting out of the car was painful and slow. I limped into the ER. I would have accepted a ride in a wheel chair.

The ER was packed but when it came clear the shape I was in, they put me in a bed immediately. I can't describe the pain I felt, but I must have been credible because a male nurse came by and gave me a shot of morphine. It was a dose of heaven.

They took an X-ray of my lungs then wheeled me out of the ER into a double room. There was another patient in there, on the other side of a screen, who I never saw. I know he was there because his snoring sounded like a jackhammer. I can't say much good about the staff. I'm not one to complain about doctors, nurses and the other people who clean things and bring you things, but this bunch wouldn't answer my call. You might think I was pushing the buzzer every five minutes. I wasn't. They were, looking back, unprofessional.

An hour or so later a guy came into the room holding a chart. I don't *think* he was a doctor. Maybe he was a nurse.

"Your lungs are perfectly clear," he said. "You have a little curvature of the spine. Has it occurred to you that you could have a pinched nerve? Pain like yours that you say comes in waves can be a pinched nerve."

I didn't answer. I *couldn't* answer. Whatever had ahold of me was bigger than a pinched nerve. I knew *that* much.

Monday morning Sandy helped me into a bathtub of warm water. Important point: August Spivey does *not* take a sponge bath. He showers, and when no shower is available, he will allow himself a bath. But no one, *NO ONE,* cleans August Spivey with a washcloth and a pan of sudsy water. Such treatment is for old people or little kids and I am neither.

I was in that hospital three days. After a stay in a hospital you hope things are improving but I was getting worse. I could tell. And I was right. On Wednesday morning, a black man in a long white lab-coat came in my room with a pair of Mexican nurses. I didn't get his name. He had a doctor look. He walked and talked with authority and the two nurses answered *"yes sir"* after everything he directed.

"Get this man *anything* he wants," he ordered.

"Morphine," I whispered.

The black doctor left and I got my morphine. It didn't help me sleep, but it cut the pain way down to a tolerable level.

That afternoon the black doctor came in the room with the same two nurses. Sandy wasn't there but I was awake and understood what he said.

"We don't have here what it takes to help you."

"Cancer?" I asked.

"No," he answered, "it's called an empyema."

"Surgery?" I asked.

He nodded, *"Yes."*

The ambulance ride to the Catholic hospital was smooth. The siren wasn't blaring, but it wasn't that kind of ride. The morphine had worn off and I was suffering but I knew I was going to a hospital where I would get some real help.

When I arrived at the hospital there was a room waiting for me. There was no dillydallying around. I didn't know what was wrong with me, but I knew it couldn't be good. I was scared. I figured I was dying and they wanted

Sandy there with me when they gave me the bad news; but they could've done that at the other hospital. I couldn't tell if I was coming or going.

A nurse followed me into my room. She was stout with blond hair and looked about forty. It crossed my mind that she was experienced. She looked at my chart, picked up the phone next to my bed, and called *the man.*

By *the man* I mean Dr. Pane. Make that Dr. Dean Pane who I found out later was one of the big dogs for treating what I had gnawing on my lung.

"Doctor Pane," she said standing next to me, "we have a real problem here. This is a bad one. Ok, we're moving him right now on to ICU."

She made a quick call to her crew: a second nurse and two black orderlies. They wheeled me in my bed down the hall. I watched the ceiling tiles click by. I heard trays and silverware clattering on metal. I figured it must be dinner time but I'd lost my appetite days ago. A pair of doors made a *whoosh* sound. I was in ICU.

The gang who rolled me into ICU dressed me in hospital clothes and left the room. I was pulling in tiny puffs of air, but I couldn't call it breathing. I ached all over. *The enamel on my teeth hurt.*

In a while a man walked into the room. He held an X-ray up to the fluorescent light above my bed. He was thin, average height, red-haired, wearing blue jeans and a cowboy hat. He looked to be in his mid-fifties.

"You don't have to talk," he said to me," but nod if you can hear me."

I nodded.

"Do you know what an empyema is?"

I shook my head slightly. He held the X-ray up to the light so we both could see it.

"You don't only have pneumonia. Your lung is

infected. It's coated with a gelatinous cone about an inch thick." He pointed with his index finger at the crust which engulfed my left lung. "You're going into surgery tomorrow morning at six. Do you understand that?"

I nodded and he left the room. The ICU team came back in and went to work on me. I noticed a monitor at the end of my bed. Electrodes were hooked to my fingers and the green screen on the monitor reacted. I'd seen enough TV-medicine to know that if the line that ran across it went flat, I was dead. I saw peaks and valleys running left to right that let me know I wasn't in Heaven or Hell or the Catholic Purgatory where I was probably headed someday.

Then the tubes went in. They all helped a lousy day *feel* worse. One went down my nose, another, a long tube, was worked through my mouth and down my throat. The third one was an intravenous needle that went into my wrist. I got groggy fast. A sleeping potion was OK with me. The last one was connected to a part of me that lurks behind a zipper and doesn't get much fresh air.

I was fully hooked up and left alone. I liked the silence, interrupted only by the sound of air compressing into, I assume, my failing lung. I still didn't quite understand what an empyema was. The guy in the cowboy hat, probably Dr. Pane, gave me a quick lesson in lung anatomy, but I didn't know if I was coming out of this or not. With nothing but time or maybe eternity ahead of me it occurred to me I'd been sick since August; four months of snot, sore throat, fever and worn-out breathing. Was I afraid of death? I had enough of a survival instinct to want to live. And God? Who knew? Jack says you eventually separate *what* you believe from what you *want* to believe. He says *faith* is believing in what hasn't been proven up, and *hope* is *wanting* to believe in what you can't prove. Jack says his faith comes and goes, but he's *always hoped* there is a God. In my opinion, Jack does way too much thinking on the subject.

Before I went under I got a brief glimpse of the hallway outside the ICU. A nurse walked through those doors that made the *whoosh* sound and I saw afternoon sunlight splash on the floor and part way up the wall. That made me feel better. Sun always encourages me. November had been grey and windy and generally crummy. If I was going to die, my last look at life was a happy one.

But I didn't die. I came out of my coma with what felt like a big oily snake uncoiling itself in my stomach, then crawling up my throat and out my mouth.

"Blow out, Mr. Spivey! Blow out!"

I felt hands on my back holding me upright in a bed. Someone was pulling at that snake that was living in my guts. I coughed and exhaled as I was told. It hurt at first, but then I inhaled a deep hit of air I hadn't enjoyed in months. It was sweet. I didn't know breathing could feel so good. God bless oxygen!

I was weak as a kitten but able to eat real food. Sandy was in the room. I took it slow. A small plate of scrambled eggs, toast, and a strip of bacon washed down by cold orange juice made it worthwhile being human. That afternoon Dr. Pane came to visit.

"Where's the cowboy hat?" I asked. He smiled at that.

"Left it in the car," he said.

He lifted my gown and pointed to a bandage on my left rib cage.

"We had to install a shunt into that lung. We got the infectious cone scraped away. There was plenty of it. It filled up a container the size of a mixing bowl. But your lung kept filling up with liquid. So, we had to drain that left lung twice."

"So, it was serious?" I asked.

"Oh yes," he confirmed, "you were on the fence Thursday and Friday night. It could have gone either way."

I stayed in the Catholic hospital three more days. That totaled fifteen days (three in the local hospital, twelve in the Catholic hospital, of which nine of those days were in ICU) I had been on my back. Physical therapy was rough. My legs and arms felt like noodles. I had absolutely no strength at first in either. Twice a day I used a walker, with the therapist holding onto a belt fastened around my waist, to go up and down the hall outside my room. The first few times I went down to my knees out of breath. Staff had to help me up.

The morning of my discharge an orderly pushed me in a wheelchair to the front of the hospital. After four more days of relearning to walk, I was getting the strength back in my arms and legs. Sandy picked me up in her car. I lifted myself from the wheel chair. The orderly, a young strong black man, held my arm while I walked slowly but surely to the passenger side of Sandy's car.

I was under doctors' orders to take it easy for six weeks. The lung was working, but needed time to heal. And the hole where the shunt had been inserted needed healing as well. Every so often I would cough from my spot on the couch and my chest would hurt, reminding me of what I went through. Once a day Sandy and I took Luther for a walk around our block. It normally took twenty minutes or so, sometimes with me stopping for air. I was getting stronger by the day, my lung was healing, the shunt-hole itching (a good sign). And my appetite had returned. I didn't realize to what extent I'd lost my sense of taste and smell (in the hospitals) which killed my appetite. Sandy began making me three square meals a day; bacon, eggs, pancakes for breakfast; hamburgers and salads for lunch;

fajitas and baked chicken for dinner. I was getting the twenty pounds I'd lost back. I was hungry as a wolf in winter.

After a week at home, Jack came to see me. He'd been to the Catholic hospital during my stay in ICU. I don't remember the visit since I was unconscious during that time. He said he stood at the foot of my bed watching the green monitor and hoping the white line wouldn't go flat.

"Jack," I said, "I saw Quinn." Sandy was at work, Luther was on the floor not three feet away, Jack stood in the living room facing me, the darkened television at his back.

"Come again," said Jack.

"I saw Quinn."

"Quinn's dead, Augie."

"I know that, Jack."

Quinn Gallagher and I met over a fist fight at our neighborhood park when we were twelve. We beat hell out of each other and after that were close as brothers. Quinn was one tough little bastard. He'd fight with a brick wall if he thought it looked at him funny. Like a lot of my pals, Quinn was dead early.

"I still don't get it, Augie," said Jack.

"I saw the other side, Jack. Or at least the front end of it."

I could tell Jack's wheels were turning. That *faith/hope* dilemma was eating at him.

"That was the medication," he said.

"No, Jack, it was real. I saw Quinn."

"What was he doing?" asked Jack.

"He was in a white room."

"The hospital's white, Augie," Jack interrupted.

"Jack, you're not hearing me. It was real. The room was white. *All white*. Quinn was there, waiting for me."

"What did he look like?" asked Jack.

"Like he did before he died. A grown up. He looked peaceful. I had no reason to think he was tormented."

"What did he say?"

"Nothing. He didn't say anything. He was expressionless, he was waiting for me to decide."

"Decide what, Augie?"

"If I wanted to come over or not. It was my choice to live or die."

Jack left. I don't know if he believed me or not. I didn't care. I *knew* who and what I saw. What I didn't tell Jack is what happened after that. Just before I came out of my coma in ICU, I went out of body. I hovered over my hospital bed. I saw myself with the hospital staff, Doctor Pane, the nurse who took care of me in ICU, and the orderlies standing in a group around my bed, them holding me forward, pounding on my back, screaming, "Blow out, Mr. Spivey! Blow out!" Then I got sucked back into my body. It wasn't nice and gentle. I *dove* back into my body. And it made a noise, a loud crazy noise like someone rubbing hard on the surface of balloon full of air.

I continued healing, keeping my story to myself. I didn't share it with anyone other than Jack. Things got a little better. Sandy and I don't go out often. We live on a tight budget, but we needed out of the house, a night to celebrate. We went to one of our favorite restaurants, *Lupe Comida,* not far from our place. I ate big. I had two cheese enchiladas smothered in picante sauce, flour tortillas and guacamole to *live* for.

On the way out of the restaurant who should I run into but Dr. Pane with a woman about his age and a small boy with red hair.

"Doing OK, Mr. Spivey?" he asked. He stuck out his hand which I gripped but followed with a bear hug that shook him. He was a little uneasy, then laughed, as did his wife and child once he introduced me.

"Anybody who rescues August Spivey from death's door gets a hug," I said.

But the insomnia wouldn't go away. It was lack of sleep, I'm sure, that was behind my cold and eventual near death. Without money, I worried constantly. I took a hit on my undercover income, hoping the quality of my work could get me back in the hotels. Attorneys and their paralegals, on the other hand, were a different problem. They *don't care* if you're sick. They move onto the next guy. Court dates are time-sensitive. The law-firm people are constantly under the gun which puts paper servers like me *under the gun.* It's hard to get back in with a paralegal if he or she drops you from their queue.

I had an idea. I didn't let my lawsuit-paper clients know I was recovering from a serious illness. I kept accepting the papers, about thirty a month, and contacted Chuckie Mays. Chuckie has saved my neck more than I've saved his. He knew about my situation. Sandy, at my direction, called him. He dropped in.

"Chuckie, the money's all yours. I count thirty papers, twenty or more are easy serves. Doctors, lawyers, corporate higher-ups. There are five or six in bad country. You know, manufactured homes, pit bulls, that stuff."

"I'll take them all, Augie, and we'll split the money down the middle. That's how you and me do business."

It went down like we agreed. Chuckie came through like the biting sow he is. Batman has nothing on Chuckie Mays. He shakes your hand, looks you in the eye, it's money in the bank.

13

A PAIR OF ANN MARGARETS

I like to get them early. Before they leave for work. Before they can avoid me. I get them early and my whole day goes better. I don't get them early, things get harder.

The easiest ones to serve are the professionals: doctors and accountants who don't get rattled when a lawsuit comes calling at their door. They have money. They usually have a lawyer. Or, if they don't have one, they can afford one.

Poor guys aren't easy to serve. I show up on the porch, they think they're in trouble or owe somebody money. And you know what? I guess they're right. I usually bring bad news.

The hardest people to serve are black women and young Mexican men. Any time I go east of the freeway, I know it could get rough. Black women think I'm a cop or a bill collector. The Mexican guys have that macho thing going. Once they figure out I'm not a cop it's a steady stream of bad-ass attitude. Give me white professionals in their cozy, rich homes any day.

I got a call from a lawyer named Mike Buck. Or, I should say, I called him. Mike has a big heart. He's also got a little-man's complex. He wears a cowboy hat that makes him seem taller. Take the ten gallons away, you think the floor's talking to you.

Mike and I go back a long way. He's never stiffed me. I can't say that for all lawyers. I like him. I'm loyal to him. For him, I'll go the extra distance. Some servers do the minimal work. They make one attempt at service, and then they submit their affidavit requesting substitute-service. I don't do that with any lawyer I serve for, especially Mike Buck. I make at least three attempts before I go the substitute-service route. Mike Buck was one of my first customers back when I didn't know the trade. I made a lot of mistakes, but Mike was patient. I taught myself the process business one step at a time. Trial and error. Now, I'm one of the best. I'd guess I've delivered five-thousand papers. To my knowledge not one's been kicked back to me. I'm proud of that. The whole time I was learning, Mike Buck was good to me. God Bless Mike Buck!

"Augie," said Buck, "I'm sorry I didn't get by to see you."

I shrugged, "That's OK, Mike. We're not hospital pals."

"Yeah," said Buck, "but still... So, it was pneumonia?"

"It was," I said," but it was also an empyema. It's like a beehive of snot and infection that coats the outside of your lung. Makes it very hard to breath."

"I heard," said Buck, "you were touch-and-go."

"I was told that," I said.

Buck leaned forward in his chair.

"You see anything?"

"When?" I asked.

"When you were close to death," said Buck.

"Yeah," I said, "I saw a few things."

Mike was religious. He loved to talk about this stuff. And it was true.

"I went out of body," I said.

"No shit?"

"Really."

"What was it like?" asked Buck.

"I hovered."

"Over your body?"

"Yeah."

"You see anything else?" he asked.

"Like what?"

"Well, like the light."

"No light," I said.

"But you hovered."

"Yes, I said I did."

"And when you were done hovering?" asked Buck.

"I slammed back into my body. It made a big, popping sound. Like snapping your fingers real sharp."

"Whew!" said Buck.

He leaned back in his chair. From behind a stack of files I barely saw the top of his head.

"Augie," he said, "you didn't call me."

"I was sick," I said.

"No," said Buck, "I'm talking about not calling me *before* the pneumonia."

"I know that. I was sick before I had the pneumonia and the empyema," I corrected.

"Too sick to answer your phone?"

"Yeah," I said. "Too sick."

Mike got quiet. He normally had a shotgun for a mouth. When he stopped talking it meant his wheels were turning.

"You don't think I can get him served, do you?" I asked.

"Augie, I need this. I can't have you dropping out on me."

"I won't do that, Mike."

"Neal Green is his lawyer," said Buck.

"Good. I've served paper for him. He knows me."

"Then you know that he doesn't miss anything. I'm not sure about this, Augie."

"Mike, I'll put it in the guy's hand."

"You better," said Buck. "You better."

He took a file off the stack on his desk. He opened the file and tossed me a pair of photographs.

"That's my client," said Buck. "She's suing for divorce."

"Hmm," I said. "Reminds me of Ann Margaret back when Ann was inspirational."

"A little," said Buck. "I can see that."

The woman in the picture looked to be about forty. She had red hair and was easy to stare at.

"And this," said Buck, "is her husband."

I took the picture from Buck. The guy in it was blond, blue-eyed, curly- haired and Arian to the max.

"This isn't one of those 'we can still be friends' deals," said Buck. "This is very nasty."

"How bad?" I asked.

"Well, she's in South Dakota, afraid of him. She and I e-mail one another. She was very careful about giving me her phone number which is unlisted. She tells me I'm the only one who has her address."

"Kids?" I asked.

"No kids. This is all about property. She wants half. He doesn't want to give her anything."

"He's violent?" I asked.

"She says he is," said Buck. "He's a gun-guy. Thinks the Second Amendment is the whole Constitution. Thinks everybody but him is a Communist."

"A redneck," I estimated.

"No, he's no hillbilly," said Buck. "He's some sort of contractor. Owns his own construction business. And from what his wife says, a major-league, control-freak. You can do this, Augie?"

"Yes," I said.

"You're sure? Don't bullshit me."

"Like I said, Mike. I'll put it in his hand."

On the way out I stopped at Dina Toomey's desk. Dina is Mike's administrative girl. In a small office like Mike's she does everything. I make it a point to be good to the girls who work in these offices. Truth be known, if they don't like you, you don't get any paper to serve. They like you, you get the paper.

I know as much as I can about Dina. I study her desktop. I see a Starbucks cup on her desk, I bring her a Starbucks gift-card a couple of times a year. Dina's birthday doesn't get by me without a card and a little something in it.

Dina's what you call a *plus-size*. The last time I saw her, three years ago, she was big and she'd only gotten bigger. Needless to say, she brings a load of personality to the table. She's also one of the kindest people I've met. In this world, that makes her rare.

"We all thought you died and went to Heaven," she said.

"Sometime," I said, "I'll tell you all about Heaven."

She handed me a parcel of papers held together with a paper clip. In it were the citation and return along with the petition styled *Mary Breuder, Plaintiff v. Gary Breuder, Defendant.*

"Gary Breuder," I read.

"Pronounced Brider," said Dina.

"You know this because…?"

"That's what Mike says."

I pointed to the Rolodex on Dina's desk.

"Am I still in there?"

"Let's see," she said. She scrolled down to my name and then held it up for me to see. "This is still correct?"

"It is," I confirmed.

She set the Rolodex down.

"So what happened to you?" she asked.

"All sorts of stuff," I said. "But I'm back now. Are you and I good?"

"Yes, we are," she said. "Just like you were never gone."

I thanked her for that.

"How long you been working for Buck?" I asked.

"Too long," she answered.

"You gonna stay here forever?" I asked.

She nodded toward Mike's door which was shut.

"It looks like it."

"How about you?" she asked.

"What about me?"

"How long you been a private eye?"

"Well, let's see," I said. "Too long."

"And you're going to do it forever?"

"It looks like it," I said.

I started to go home, get a good night's sleep, and then serve Breuder in the morning. But Dina had pointed out to me that Breuder's home was on my way. It was out in the country, not far off the interstate on a Farm-to-Market that connected with a long, private road. Mike Buck got that from Breuder's very unhappy wife. Along with the process papers, Dina gave me a drawing that showed the route from Buck's office to Breuder's place. I had no reason not to give it a shot. It was three in the afternoon. If Breuder was his own boss I might catch him at home and get this thing over.

I pulled off the interstate on to the Farm-to-Market and then settled in for a drive in the woods. Dina's map showed the private road to be seven miles from the interstate. I watched my odometer click off the miles.

Breuder's private road hit the Farm-to-Market just under seven miles. I took a right and crossed over a cattle guard through an open gate. On paper the road was a crooked line that looked a lot easier than what I got; a narrow strip of caliche, not much wider than my red Toyota pickup, lined with cedar trees on both sides. There was no break in the trees. No hint of one. No shoulder to pull onto if a car came at me from the front or the rear.

A couple of hundred feet in, the road started to zigzag. Whoever built it had it in mind to mess with strangers. I crept along at no more than ten miles an hour, the cedar branches scraping along the top and sides of my truck. From his picture and Buck's description of him, Breuder didn't come across to me as an economy-truck sort of guy. Other than a few spots of sunlight on the caliche, I was in a dark tunnel of trees not knowing if at the next turn I would drop off into a gully or a ditch. I had this lousy thought that I would take a header into a creek bed and lay there until some archeologist came along in a million years or so and found me in my dirtied trousers. When I get this way, scared shitless I mean, I tell myself it's just as easy to go forward as it is to back up. That's a load of bullshit, but it's what I feed on.

After a mile, the road opened into a clearing marked by a NO TRESPASSING sign at the foot of a driveway. Several acres had been cleared. Inside what looked like an electric fence sat a barn to the left and across from it a single-story, ranch-style house. Both buildings, the yard, and the cleared land were *Grade A* nice and neat. The kind of place I think about when I want to be far away.

Twenty years ago, I'd have walked up on the house like I was a delivery boy dropping off candy and flowers. Now, I pay very close attention to where I am. I see an SUV parked in the driveway, maybe has a baby seat in the back, I know I'm dealing with those professionals I like so much. If there's a water bowl on a porch or a few piles of dog shit scattered here and there, I know man's best friend is probably in the area. You give me some young guy, who doesn't fit in, has a few brain cells to rub together, I could teach him this work. He's all the raw material I'd need.

I knocked on a piece of wood most of us couldn't afford. The door opened. A woman stepped out on the porch. She was red-haired. Like the woman in the photograph she reminded me of Ann Margaret. At first I thought it was the same woman but this one was much younger and with Father Time in her corner, fresher looking.

"Oh no," she said, "was Gary expecting this?"

"Is he here?" I asked.

"No. Would you like to come in and wait?"

I could have handed her the paper and fudged on my affidavit but I promised Mike Buck I'd put it in Breuder's hand.

"No," I said. "He'll be back in a while?"

"Yes, you know, I just have to say something."

"What's that?" I asked.

"This is so unfair to Gary."

I didn't say anything because I didn't care.

"His wife has made up so much about him. He's really gentle."

I handed her my card, a cute little thing with a logo that made me look more important than I was.

"Wait a minute," she said.

She disappeared into the house. A minute later she returned with one of Breuder's business cards.

"Those are Gary's numbers. If you could just meet him you'd see that he's a great guy. Are you sure you wouldn't like to come in?"

I looked around, past the wire fence into the thick cedar. I can bullshit right along with the next guy. But when it's time to do business, I get professional. I keep things short. No small-talk. No chit-chat. This girl, on the other hand, had a friendly streak that was hard to pass up.

"You guys are really remote out here," I commented.

"Yes, we are" she agreed. "I didn't think I'd like it."

"I bet it gets dark."

"My, yes! So dark you can't see anything unless the moon's full. Truthfully, I really don't think Gary would mind if you came in."

"If I go get gas, and then come back, he'll be home?"

"Oh, I think so," she said.

I turned to walk back to my truck.

"We had some sort of problem out here last night," she said. "It got me and Gary a little edgy."

"What was that?" I asked. She made edgy look good.

"I don't know for sure."

She pointed beyond the fence, off into the cedar.

"There's a fellow who lives back over in there. Something happened. Gary will know."

I drove back down that twisted crazy road listening for anything that sounded like an engine. I counted the turns, eighteen of them, before things straightened out. I filled my truck with *regular* at a gas station where the Farm-to Market connected with the interstate then found some shade for a ten-minute nap. An hour later Breuder's road didn't have me quite so much by the balls. There's a lesson in everything.

I stopped short of the driveway with the NO TRESPASSING sign in full view. An F-150 pickup was parked on the drive midway between the barn and the house. Unless he had another way in, I saw no way Breuder could get a truck that size through the cedar. I took five or six steps onto the property thinking by now his girlfriend had gotten him ready for me.

"STOP! STOP! RIGHT THERE! STOP NOW!" I heard come from near the F-150.

"Civil process," I said.

From behind that truck rushed a man I figured to be Breuder. He stopped within thirty feet of me, aiming a pistol at my face.

"Civil process," I yelled. "Civil fucking process."

I heard a pop. I thought a bullet going over my head might make some noise, maybe like bacon sizzling in a pan, but it was quiet as any silent fart I'd turned loose on mankind.

I've looked down a gun before. Once, when my battery went dead, a punk and his girlfriend picked me up hitchhiking. They pulled over in an alley and robbed me of my wallet. The other time me and a pal walked into a convenience store as it was being robbed. Me, my buddy, and a mouthy Vietnamese clerk got marched into the cooler. In Houston, the cooler is where you usually take a bullet in the back of the head. I said the Lord's Prayer on that one and came out of it OK. Until now, no live bullet had ever come my way.

"Gary! Gary!" It was the girlfriend's voice coming from my right. "Gary. Have you lost your mind? He's a delivery guy for Crissake!"

I glanced over at the girlfriend who was standing on the porch. That Ann Margaret face of hers looked like it was having a charley horse. I held my hands up in the air expecting Breuder to come to his senses. He kept the gun aimed directly into my face.

"Civil process," I said as calmly as I could.

"I don't give a shit who you are," he huffed.

From as close as we stood, I could hear him breathe. It was that yoga stuff, in through the nose, out through the mouth. The kind of breathing gentle folk do just before they blow your brains out.

"I'm gone," I said, keeping my hands way up in the air.

I stepped backward off the driveway onto the caliche. With my left hand in the air, I used my right to open the truck. Once I got inside I kept my left hand on the dash while I used the right hand again to start up the ignition. I hadn't convinced Breuder I meant no harm. He kept the gun leveled at me. I couldn't blame a guy who lived in the middle of nowhere for not trusting a stranger. But I was no threat. Breuder was the nut-job Mike Buck said he was. I backed my truck in reverse down the cedar-lined road.

Fear didn't set in until later that night. Everything I do now seems to go in slow-motion. Food doesn't digest as fast as it once did. I don't shit but every second or third day. Maybe old turds like me take longer to get scared.

I turned on ESPN. The Yankees and Baltimore were playing. I sat and watched, thinking if you gotta work there's no better job than baseball. My wife, Sandy, came in and sat down on the couch. Sandy likes those remodel shows where a couple of gay guys come in and change up your home. For Sandy, and only Sandy, I'll switch channels. She's the only person on the planet willing to understand me. I could tell, that she could tell, that I was scared.

"Look," I said, "I know I'm whacky. I don't go around thinking I'm normal and everybody else is messed up."

"I know that," said Sandy.

"So?"

"So, there must be something else."

"Like what?" I asked. "Can you think of anything right here, right now, I can do?"

"Of course, not. Not at this minute."

"I'm not going back to bartending. And I'm not going off to some technical school."

"But why is it so important to serve him personally?"

"Because Mike Buck thinks I lost my nerve, that's why. And you know what? I think I have. Private eye is what I do. It's the only thing I can do."

Sandy let out a sigh. Her way of letting me know the Berlin wall was going up. We went back to watching TV. A team of tailgaters was turning a dump into a nice set of digs.

"So what are you going to do?"

"I'm going to get him served," I said.

"Augie, he'll shoot you."

"No he won't. I got an idea."

My dad sold cars. He sold good. I never missed a meal. He asked me once if I could sell a five-hundred-dollar car for five-thousand dollars and not feel bad about it. I assured him no way I could do that. He assured me no way I could sell for a living.

I sold Sandy good. I sold myself better. I'd get this creep served. I'd call those numbers on his business card. I'd let him know I was just doing my job. I'd let him meet me some place public. Or I'd park myself where his road met the Farm-To-Market. I'd be nice. I'd be polite. I'd expect the same from him. If he didn't show up, or got pissy with me, I'd file charges on him for the shot he took at me. And I'd sue his fake, cowboy-ass for assault. I'd make his divorce seem like a walk on the beach.

"But you were on his land," said Sandy.

"Doesn't mean he can fire a gun at me."

"Are you sure about that?"

"Sure enough to be a prick over the phone and feel good about it."

"What if he says he never shot at you? Your word against his, right?"

"His word against mine and the girlfriend's," I said.

"She won't turn on him," said Sandy. "Women don't turn on their men. Not if they have a good thing going."

"Yeah, maybe, we'll see," I said. "After today, her thing might not seem so good."

An hour later Mr. Insomnia cuddled up in bed with me and Sandy. Here's how he does business: He books a room in your head. He won't leave. He turns little things into big things, one thing into a lot of things. He piles idea on top of idea. One minute you ask yourself if you should get up to take a piss, three hours later you think the Russians have their missiles pointed at this great country of ours and it's your job to call it in.

I didn't sleep two winks. Neither did Sandy. I stayed awake all night listening to her think. She stayed awake listening to me. That's the way it is when you're each married to a worrier.

I got up at five thirty in the morning and dressed. I let Sandy sleep. She'd finally fallen under. I left her a note that told her I love her. For guys who don't know, that's money in the bank.

Out in the kitchen I ate a banana, and then drank a cup of hot, black coffee. I always go light at breakfast. Most times, I don't eat lunch. I save my big meal for dinner. It's my way of celebrating all things big and small. I'd love to sit down to a plate of ham and eggs, maybe some gravy and biscuits and picture my cells soaking up all that nutrition. In my work, me against the world, it pays to stay hungry. A little gnaw in the gut keeps me just the right amount of pissed-off.

I made a pair of phone calls to Breuder's two numbers. Both times I left messages on his answering machines. Both times I niced-it-up a little. I decided to give myself twenty-four more hours to get him served. By tomorrow morning, if I didn't have him served, I'd tell Mike Buck to turn things over to a constable.

I had some errands that needed running so Breuder, I told myself, would have to wait on me. I paid my fees at the Private Eye Board. I dropped in on a couple of law offices just to let them know Augie Spivey was back in the rotation. Some of the girls remembered me, a few didn't know me from Adam. I was starting all over again.

About the time I was scheduled to miss lunch, my cell phone rang. When I'm at home, I don't answer the phone. I let the answering machine do what it's supposed to. The way I see it, ninety-nine percent of what people say can wait. My cell phone rings, that's different. My cell phone rings, I answer it. It was Breuder, insisting we meet at a public place.

"Public places are my favorite places," I said.

We agreed to meet in the parking lot where I had bought gas. It was a good fit; out in the open, where the interstate met the Farm-to-Market, a wide, concrete apron with ten sets of pumps, a bright, clean convenience store, and plenty of people coming and going. Working in a convenience store wouldn't be so bad if almost getting killed in one didn't mess with my head.

"You think I'm crazy?" asked Breuder. Up close, with his breather running, I thought he might be catching a cold.

"It crossed my mind," I said. "Here, you're served." He took the paper from me.

"My wife has me painted the bad-guy in this. I'm not."

"You fooled me," I said.

"Let me finish," requested Breuder.

"Go ahead. I practice a little psychology on the side."

He launched into how his wife had threatened to kill him if he left her. How what went on over at the neighbor's had him and his girlfriend spooked.

"So, you got a dog?" I asked.

"Yeah," he answered.

"I didn't see him yesterday," I said.

"In that respect, you were a little lucky."

He went on to tell me his neighbor, a loner, had died of a heart attack. There was noise coming from beyond the trees the night before. It wasn't until the next afternoon, not long before I got there, that he and his girlfriend found out about the death. Earlier that morning, his dog, a Doberman named "Orbit," had come trotting up to the house, his muzzle lathered up in blood. Orbit had been doing some eating.

"So, dead guy, bloody dog, crazy wife says she's out to get you. Yeah, I can see why you might be a little jumpy."

"We're OK on this?" he asked.

"You're forgiven," I said. I felt like giving him a bunch of Hail Mary's to say, but I didn't want him getting mad at me again.

I shook the hand that shot at me.

I drove home with the windows down. I felt pretty good. I was back in the game. I'd make Mike Buck happy. I'd have Dina Toomey in my corner. I'd put Sandy at ease for a while. That was plenty. Once, I lived for recognition but now I was happy being famous in small circles.

But I should have felt real good and didn't. Getting shot at scared me. I didn't see that going away. Yeah, I came close to death with the pneumonia. And, I went out-of-body. No kidding. None of that made a philosopher out of me. I want to go to Heaven but I don't want to die.

The one I couldn't figure was the girlfriend, Ann Margaret Number Two. The one who invited me in. She seemed smart. Smart enough to get a job or keep away from a guy like Breuder. Maybe she was one of those girls who needed a guy, any guy, to feel good about herself. One thing I know, you've got to manage your lonely. You don't, it will eat you up. Maybe she was just doing a little of that.

14

LONELY WORLD

I hadn't heard from Chuckie Mays in over a month. That worried me a little because Chuckie and I were supposed to have lunch a week ago and Chuckie doesn't miss appointments.

I called over to his place where I got no answer. So, I checked with Candi, his Asian-stewardess girlfriend who flies in and out of town just enough to keep the two of them happy. Candi told me Chuckie was in one of his bipolar-sleepless periods, and the best thing to do was leave him alone. I like Candi, she's fun to look at and think about, but when it comes to advice, she serves peanuts and ginger ale at twenty-thousand feet for a reason.

I knocked on Chuckie's door. Chuckie lives in a manufactured home I'm sure he'll never get paid off in a trailer park that's the only place the Chuckie Mayses of this world can live.

I beat near hell on the door until I heard a groan that sounded faintly like, "Come the fuck in if it's that important." I found Chuckie laid up on the couch looking like the losing side in a bad war. The way Chuckie told it, he hadn't slept in four days.

"What's your record?" I asked.

"This ties it," he said, "and this is not something you should make a joke out of."

And that was true. I, with my own sleep problems, had no business seeing only the lighter side of Chuckie's nocturnal predicament.

"You want me to get that?" I asked.

The phone was ringing loud and clear, begging for somebody to shut it up but Chuckie waved me off.

"Let it roll. I'm in no shape to take any work."

So, Chuckie and I listened while his answering machine recorded the message of one Tommie Jones, paralegal for *Jenson and Kaiser,* a downtown law firm with a beautiful view of the city. Tommie had a guy's name but an abundance of female talent everywhere else. I'd worked for her plenty of times. She pretty much ran *J and K.* The partners all loved her. The rest of the staff, the young lawyers included, didn't cross her. She was the queen-bitch who could get you fired. She left a message on Chuckie's recorder that made it clear if he didn't get a witness name of Bobby Pipes subpoenaed and in the courtroom of Judge Harold Miller by three that afternoon, he'd never serve another paper for her again. And that meant he'd never serve another paper for at least ten or twelve other law firms around town so great was the reach of Tommie Jones.

Chuckie raised up slow and stiff in a way that would've made Lazarus look fit. He sat for a minute with his head between his hands talking personal to the carpet.

"Christ, I'm fucking psychotic and now if I wanna stay in business I gotta serve some jack-fuck two hundred feet up in the air."

I gave him a nice little scratch on the back, nothing soft and girlie, more like the monkey-rub your old man gave you when you and he were wrestling on the floor.

"That's why I'm here, Chuckie."

See, Chuckie and I got us an agreement. One of us can't run his paper, the other one will. That way we keep the lawyers and their paralegals happy. Because in this business there is no loyalty. You run through a wall for a lawyer, put yourself in harm's way so he can hold up his end of due process, it makes no difference to any of those pricks that you're sick as a dog and can't answer the bell one time, *one fucking time.* It's all about "what have you done for me lately?"

I don't pack a gun. Sometimes I wish I did. I could if I so chose. The State of Texas made it legal when it bestowed upon me my investigator's license. But guns scare me. When my brother, Jack, and I were kids I almost shot him with our uncle's .22. A flock of birds flew by and I took a wild shot over the top of Jack's head. Six inches lower, my brother's dead or drooling.

But Chuckie does carry a gun. I've seen it. He carries it around his ankle. I don't know what model it is because I don't know guns. But it will put you on your back forever, of that I'm sure. It was taking target practice that he and Candi met. Chuckie's as tough as they come when he's on his game. So, when he shakes my hand a little too long and gets misty around the eyes I know he's worried, seriously worried, about his private eye livelihood.

"August, thank you. I mean it."

"I know you do," I said.

I took the subpoena and gave it a quick once-over. Bobby Pipes worked construction where the old airport was being converted into a village of retail outlets and top-end apartment living. He was an unwilling witness to a lawsuit that had his cousin being sued for smacking an old man. Pipes saw the whole thing. It was noon, I had to get Pipes into court by three o'clock or Chuckie Mayes would have a very mad paralegal on his hands.

I drove out to the construction site where Pipes worked. It was crawling with hard-hats, hammering, hauling, living in their sweat.

"You want him, he's up there."

A big redneck foreman, who could've been a bad-guy in any western, pointed to a crane that went up at least two-hundred feet in the air.

"I gotta serve him," I said.

"So, go get him."

"Can you call him down?"

"Could, but today you're shit out of luck,"

"Why you say that?" I asked.

"I guess you just caught me in a pissy mood."

I've met a few construction foremen in my work; every one of them's been a mean asshole. A guy's nice to me, I'm nice back. A guy's a prick, he gets my negativity. And a guy wants to fight, we can settle things that way. I won't start a fight, but I won't back down. Only time I backed down, I was twenty when an older guy, looked about forty, pulled a knife on me. I never had something so serious waved in my face. I saw the bastard a couple of years later in the parking lot of a grocery store. He was carrying a six-pack under each arm and looked as drunk then as the day he got knife-happy. It crossed my mind to start up where he and I left off, but I let it go. Wisdom is not a bad thing. I let the booze do my getting even for me. I doubt he's alive today. By now, I figure his liver has dripped out his ass.

I passed on the foreman. I had a subpoena to serve for a pal who hadn't slept in a long time.

"How do I get up there?"

"That cage."

He pointed to a long, narrow tube a football field away. I walked across the site, dodged a front-end loader, then stepped on a metal platform and pushed a button. The ride up was slow and jerky. If I'd have been looking, I would have caught a good view of the city. But I kept it straight ahead. I wanted no part of the ground below.

At the top, the basket stopped. Five feet away, running a crane, sat Bobby Pipes.

"My foreman phoned up, said you was coming," he said.

"You're served," I said.

"You got some balls coming way the fuck up here."

"It's for a pal."

"How you know I won't fuck with you on the way down?"

"I don't," I said. "I'd take that subpoena real serious. I know that judge. And he doesn't put up with bullshit."

I'd never met that judge one day in my life, but if Pipes was going to fuck with me, I was going to fuck with him.

The way down, a series of drops and quick stops, had me pissing my pants. I'm what you call multi-phobic. For instance, I have a special thing about cockroaches. Nothing scares me more than one of those filthy bastards. Deep water scares me too. I'll swim in a pool, but you won't find me in a river or the ocean. And then there's heights. I get no satisfaction looking down from above.

On the ground, I made hard-eyes with the big redneck. I looked up at the top of the crane, then I looked at him and shrugged like it was all a big piece of chocolate cake.

I called Tommie Jones and let her know Pipes got the subpoena. She asked me why Chuckie Mays hadn't served him. I told her Chuckie had three other papers going that day, that he farmed out Pipes to me.

"He's going to show?" she asked.

"I don't know," I said. "I put the paper in his hand." It was 2:00.

She put me on hold. A few minutes later she came back.

"He called to say he's on his way. Where do I send the money?"

"Send it to Chuckie Mays," I said.

I ran over to Chuckie's to break the good news. A phone call would have done, but I wanted to see Chuckie smile. I caught Candi coming out as I was walking up.

"Chuckie and I are thinking about me moving in here," she said.

"Good for you," I said like I meant it, but why would they mess up the good thing they had going?

"I think it would be a good idea if Chuckie started taking his mail here instead of the P. O. box twenty miles away."

"Don't do that," I said.

"Why not?"

"Because in this business you make enemies. You don't want anybody figuring out where you live. Trust me on that. And don't ever list your phone number."

I knew Chuckie, being the seasoned pro he was, wouldn't give up his cover. I didn't see him and Candi lasting long under the same roof. She got my point about keeping things confidential then rushed off to the airport. The friendly skies were calling.

I walked inside for a sit-down with Chuckie.

"I got him served," I said.

"Yeah, I know. I just got a call from Tommie Jones. Two hours ago, she was a rocket up my ass, now she's rubbing on me like a cat. You want some of my action, August?"

"No, you keep it all. You'll do the same for me someday."

"August, I want to thank you."

Chuckie and I were sitting at his kitchen table. He had just polished off a chicken-fried steak with a boatload of gravy. I've never seen Chuckie eat anything green. With Chuckie, it's all fried. French fries are the closest thing he comes to vegetables. All that goo running through Chuckie's heart and it keeps beating. Go figure.

"This idea about me and Candi living together, you think it will work?"

"You want me to be nice, or tell you the truth?"

"You can be straight with me."

"I like her. She's got some naughty-girl in her. But she's not domestic and neither are you."

"See, August. That's what I like about you. You got this inner-wisdom thing going."

I fielded the compliment like I was a guy who special stuff came out of.

"August, can I ask you something?"

"Sure."

"You won't think I'm soft?"

"Don't know. Probably not."

"I need a pal."

"You mean other than Candi?"

"Yeah. You know, a guy-pal. Somebody I can bounce things off. It gets pretty lonely out here. Candi's good for some things, but not everything."

"Sure, Chuckie. I'll be your pal. You got my word on that."

I never had anybody ask me straight to pal-up. I don't plan things like that. One day it occurs to you that somebody's a pal or they're not. But I came through for Chuckie because he'd helped me plenty of times and there was enough there for me to like.

When I got home, Sandy was all broken up over a baby bluebird that didn't make it. She and I were watching it hop around in our garden for a couple of days while its mamma protected it and kept it fed. Something got to it overnight and left it in a dead little ball of feathers.

"I'm sorry he didn't make it, Sandy. I was pulling for him."

Lonely world.

15

THE LAST SIX WEEKS

I was searching for East Ramsey Street like a dentist goes digging for a rotten tooth: I wanted the job to be over, and I wanted to get paid.

Neal Green had me serving the Gillick brothers. He went through a private eye and two process servers before he got around to me. I've never dropped the ball on Neal so why he waits until the last minute to tap on me I don't know.

East Ramsey Street runs through a part of the county called "Little Appalachia." There isn't a more fucked-up piece of planet earth than those four blocks. Meth users, outdoor toilets, people with only one or two teeth in their head, and little kids who call their older sisters "mamma," that's what you find in Little Appalachia.

After you make it through Little Appalachia (*if* you make it through Little Appalachia), East Ramsey dead-ends into a twelve-unit apartment complex owned by a fella named Brian Cooper. You look up "slum lord" in the dictionary, I'm pretty sure you'll find his picture. Cooper keeps his units up one step ahead of condemnation. If you can stand rats and roaches and meth-zombies for neighbors, he's the landlord for you.

The Gillick brothers were identical twins. Gabe was about a quarter-inch taller than Gib, but you couldn't tell them apart to save your life. And to fuck with people, Gabe had Gib's name tattooed on his left arm, and Gib had Gabe's name tattooed on his right arm. You didn't know that, you might end up serving one or the other or both the wrong paper. The Gillick brothers had been served plenty of paper.

This is where life gets wackier than art. The Gillick twins, both of them, were caught up in a paternity suit by the Green sisters, Gloria and Gina, both of *them* identical twins. Gina had hooked up with Gabe in an unmatrimonial way, and Gloria had done the same with Gib. The Green sisters, if you're thinking it, were not from Little Appalachia. If they were from Little Appalachia, the Gillick twins would be married to the Green twins or the Gillicks would no longer have their male identifiers.

There are things you don't do in or near Little Appalachia: you don't go down East Ramsey after dark, you don't leave your car untended, you don't get into any bullshit with the inhabitants. I broke the first two rules since it was well after dark, and I parked my Toyota on East Ramsey.

Neal Green briefed me good on the Gillicks. I had pictures of each, and to keep things straight I had an index card that showed *Gabe/Gina* and *Gib/Gloria*.

The doors to the units were interior, which means they opened into a hall, which means I had to walk down that hall, a hall that had no lighting.

I opened the main door at the top of a porch then walked into the hall. It smelled like piss, and I figured out why the private eye and the two process servers had called "quits" on it. Ahead was one, long hall, so pitch-black you couldn't see your pecker to pee. Who knew what was down that hall? Meth-zombies toting straight razors? Angry black boys? Screw drivers? Ice picks?

A nervous kind of feeling came over me. Neal was going to owe me big on this—big enough I was going to let him know he and I were done if he passed me up again.

I called into practice a little trick the good nuns had taught me, that being the power of prayer. Two very serious and profound Hail Marys later, I was at the door of the Gillick twins. It opened.

"Mother of God!" I yelled, "Gina's in bad shape. Not gonna make it!"

"I did not harm that bitch," said the twin on the left who had "Gib" tattooed on his left arm.

I handed him the lawsuit that had Gina suing Gabe.

"And you must be Gib," I said. He had Gabe tattooed on his right arm. I gave him Gloria's lawsuit.

After the obligatory "Fuck You" from the Gillick brothers, I prayed my way back the same way I came, jumped in my truck, and drove fast as hell down East Ramsey to what I thought was a little celebration one August Spivey had coming. I called Sandy to tell her it all went good, and that if Chuckie Mays was interested, he and I could meet for a drink.

A phone call later, Chuckie and I agreed to meet at the *Torch,* a bar famous for nothing. But it was there when you needed it, and Chuckie and I liked small, out-of-the-way places a private eye couldn't get "made" in. In our business, you want anonymity.

I sat down directly at the bar which was a mistake from the second my fanny hit leather. Chuckie was coming in the door just as Willie Day, a bartender I busted about a year ago at another bar for slipping a few too-many twenties into his person, was in front of me.

"What can I get you?" he asked with a definite tone.

He gave me a major-league look over. I couldn't tell if he made me (or not) as the guy who cost him his last job. Typically, I change my look. Sometimes I go the clean-shaven route, sometimes you'll catch me with a goatee or a mustache. I alternate shirts, some dress, some casual. Same thing with pants. I wear jeans, I wear slacks. I've worn ball caps from most of the major league ball clubs or I go hatless. You won't catch me in a cowboy hat. I look silly in a cowboy hat.

"Chuckie, what you want?" I asked as Chuckie sat down.

"I'll have one of those right there." Chuckie pointed to a bottled *Miller High Life* going by on a tray.

"I'll have the same," I said, then whispered to Chuckie when Day left, "this is all I'm drinking tonight, so pay close attention to that."

Chuckie and I spent the next thirty minutes or so spinning private eye war stories. He had plenty of good ones, most I'd heard, and he'd heard most of mine, but none topped my recent journey to and from Little Appalachia.

At 11:00, we split. Chuckie and I were at the bar less than one hour. He had two beers. I had one. I gave Sandy a quick call, and told her I was on the way home. I left the parking lot with the usual sense of satisfaction that accompanies a job well-done.

I had a dreamy little drive going, all sorts of successful stuff coming and going in my very-happy state of mind. I was winding down from a scary walk in a dangerous building.

"Oh, shit," I murmured. "What the hell is this?"

A pair of cherries had come up behind me. They were big and red and had a cop to go along with them. I pulled over like any good and sober citizen would.

"Sir, please hand me your driver's license," said its driver, a serious fellow in a blue uniform.

"Certainly," I said.

I handed him what he wanted. He was typical law: meaty arms, not fat, not in shape. He was polite but had a look that said he could get instantly mean if the situation called for it.

"Step out of the car, sir."

I did that too. I knew the drill. I have been drunk behind the wheel so I knew what was coming. But this time I wasn't drunk, I hadn't been speeding. My inner bad-boy was getting a wakeup call.

"Let me see you walk this line please."

"Why?"

"Because I asked you to."

I walked the line so good Johnny Cash could've sung about me.

"That do it?" I asked.

"Now, please touch your nose with the index-finger of your left hand with your eyes closed."

"Ta Da!" I said as I completed that part of the test. I should've kept the smart-ass in me at a tolerable level but Augie Spivey was smelling a rat.

"Sir, I'm going to ask you take a breathalyzer test now."

"And I'm going to ask you to go fuck yourself."

So, that night I slept in the city's safest hotel. It's got steel bars, some of the best security you'll find anywhere, along with hookers, drunks, and various other fine-lodgers.

I used my phone call on Sandy, told her I was OK, then asked her to call Jack. Next morning Jack came by to get me out. He was his normal pisser-self, wanting to be at work, pulling all those land deals together instead of hoisting me out of a drunk tank.

"Jack, fuck you if you don't believe me on this one."

He and I talked about what was a clear-cut case of Willie Day getting even with me. No way August Spivey was going down without a fight.

"OK," Jack said, then referred me to Touchy Parks.

Touchy's real name is Gordon Parks. He went to law school with Jack. He got his name from the way he shakes hands. Touchy takes your hand with his right hand then grabs the back of your arm with his left. He holds that way far too long, the whole time looking you directly in the eye much like you were a first date. It's his signature move. Jack assures me Touchy isn't queer. He comes from a family of tactile people that believes in contact with all of mankind.

Touchy is a grade "A" litigator. He crawls up your ass and he won't come out until you call for your uncle. He's intentionally small-time. He wouldn't last one week in a big law firm and he knows it. So, he runs his own practice working primarily in the municipal and justice courts on traffic tickets and DWI. He's a mess, but he's also the mean little bastard you want in your corner when things get hard.

A couple of weeks later, Touchy and I got ready for trial. I told him Chuckie was there the night of my arrest. I laid out why Willie Day had an ax to grind with me. I wanted a trial, and I wanted it in front of my peers.

The day of trial we showed up in the court of Judge Connie Comb. Chuckie was there. So was the cop who busted me. Touchy had been in Comb's court plenty of times and told me I could expect fair and square treatment from her.

The prosecutor was a kid, so wet behind the ears you could plant corn in his collar. He swaggered in, tossed his briefcase on the table, then struck a pose that made him *look* in control. It was a bad cover-up for fear and I picked up on it right away. So did Touchy who looked happier than a mosquito in a blood bank.

"August," he said, "I won't guarantee anything, but this is looking pretty good."

Touchy and the prosecutor picked the jury. It was six people: four white guys, two white women, everybody under fifty. Touchy liked the numbers. If he had his way, he'd have all six of them be guys. He said most guys have been drunk at least once, and plenty of them more than that. I reminded him this was about me *not* being drunk.

The prosecutor's whole case was the cop. Most times, when a cop gives out a ticket or a DWI, he doesn't show so the case gets dismissed. But him showing up told me his reason for being there was more than ordinary cop-work.

The cop swore in and stated his name as officer Don Day. That did it for me. I elbowed Touchy.

"I got it," Touchy whispered. "Don't look up. Don't say anything. I'll use it."

The prosecutor let the cop tell his story. He got to the *Torch* about nine thirty and parked in a corner of the lot that gave him a good view of people leaving the bar. It wasn't the first time he'd used the *Torch* as a stake-out because of its closeness to the freeway.

He said he saw me leave at eleven and followed me to the freeway about three miles away. Once he saw me speed, he pulled me over. That's when he determined I was drunk.

Touchy went to work on him like I hoped he would. I wanted no mercy delivered upon a cop who was part of some cute little trick to fuck me over.

"So you arrived at nine-thirty and waited until eleven to follow Mr. Spivey?" asked Touchy.

"Correct."

"Any other cars leave the *Torch* between nine thirty and eleven o-clock?"

"I can't recall."

"Not one other car?"

"There may have been a few."

"But you didn't follow any of the other cars?"

"No."

"Instead, you followed Mr. Spivey for three miles, and then for a few more miles on the freeway hoping he'd do what? Speed up?"

"No. I played a hunch."

"What kind of hunch?"

"That he was drunk," said the cop.

Touchy picked up a copy of the ticket from our table.

"You've been a policeman how long?"

"Twenty years, give or take."

"Given out a few tickets?"

"A few," answered Day.

Touchy handed him the ticket.

"Officer Day, what did you write on the ticket?"

Day looked sour at the piece of paper.

"I wrote *speeding.*"

"So, Mr. Spivey was going 56 in a 55?"

"No, sir."

"He was going 57 in a 55?"

"No, sir."

"Well, then, how fast was he going?"

Day took too long to answer Touchy's question.

"You don't know what speed Mr. Spivey was going, do you, Officer Day?"

Day didn't answer. Touchy was just getting started.

"You know a bartender named Willie Day?" asked Touchy.

Day looked at his prosecutor for some help, but the kid was staring down, my guess wishing he'd gone to foot-doctor school or something just as safe like his mamma wanted.

"Yeah, I do."

"How well?"

"He's family."

"Your brother? What is he?"

"We're cousins."

"And did you talk to your cousin the day of Mr. Spivey's arrest?"

"I did."

"What time was that?"

"At night. We had a phone conversation."

"What time of night?"

"About nine, I guess."

The prosecutor finally made an objection to relevance, but by then the cop was measuring him for a new asshole. Touchy let Day go. On his way out, Day looked straight ahead. The kid was in for the butt-chewing of his life.

Chuckie Mays swore in as a witness. I knew Chuckie would show up. He and I look out for each other. Chuckie told the court we were at the *Torch* until eleven, that I had one beer, and that I made it clear that was my limit for the night. He said I left the *Torch* sober as a nun.

"You and Mr. Spivey are close friends, correct?" asked Touchy.

"We are," answered Chuckie.

"So, you'd lie for him?"

"Not under oath. I don't commit crime for anyone."

I finally got my chance. Touchy wouldn't normally put me on the stand, but he and I agreed my story needed telling.

"So, you and a bartender named Willie Day had some history?" asked Touchy.

"Yeah, I got him fired."

I went on to explain how I was a private eye who spotted Willie Day slipping money in his pocket during his shift. His former employer, another bar owner, had hired me to watch Day and two other bartenders. It cost Day his job.

"And you think bartender Day and his cousin, Officer Day, set you up?"

"I know they set me up."

"Mr. Spivey, you took a sobriety test that night?"

"I did. I passed both. I walked a very-straight line and I did that silly thing where you touch your nose."

"But you refused to take the breathalyzer. Is that correct?"

"Yes."

"Why? That was foolish, don't you think?"

"Yeah, but I was pissed off at…."

I looked at Judge Comb who flashed me a dirty look.

"I was angry at what I knew was a set-up to let the bartender get even."

Touchy leaned toward me then spoke low and serious while he looked at the jury.

"Mr. Spivey, were you drunk that night?"

"No, sir. I was not."

"Did you speed that night?"

"I hit 57 one time in a 55, but I reeled it back in immediately. I didn't do anything wrong."

The prosecutor passed on me and Chuckie. Normally, he'd grill our ass to make us look like fools or liars. But he came in unprepared thinking it would be a slam-dunk. Touchy turned him upside down.

In his closing argument, the kid went "TV lawyer." If he was a peacock, he couldn't have shown his feathers any better. He talked up big how dangerous the streets were, how society was a quilt and how everybody had to hold up his end. He told the jury it was on them to keep law and order and just because it seemed like a small trial it was still important to send a message. He was all sizzle, no steak.

Touchy spelled it out clearly for the jury. He hammered home that Willie Day had an ax to grind with me, that he and his cousin worked a game on me. I wasn't drunk, and since I wasn't speeding Officer Day had no probable cause to stop me in the first place.

The jury came back in fifteen minutes with a "not guilty." The courtroom emptied fast. I gave Touchy a big hug. Judge Comb and her bailiff left through a side door. The prosecutor came by and offered his hand to Touchy. Touchy grabbed it and held it, and held it, and held it for what seemed longer than his signature shake. But the kid didn't seem to mind.

The prosecutor left. It was Touchy and I sitting at the table. My night in Little Appalachia six weeks ago set all this into motion. I wrote Touchy a check for $500. He didn't want it since he and Jack were friends but I pushed it on him anyway.

Touchy kicked back in his chair, drinking in the air. Put together a night for Touchy with a good steak, a first-rate piece of tail, and cigars with the President in the oval office, it would all come in second to Touchy's love of the courtroom.

"Goddamn," he said. "Ain't this great?"

16

PAPER

It was eleven in the morning, Friday, when I took a call from Julietta Rojas, the girl who ran Neal Green's office. Julietta wanted me to serve a federal subpoena on Gil Timmon. Timmon was a lawyer who made his money in the world of patents, and, by my brother Jack's (himself a lawyer) normal and fair estimation, was very high up on the smart-guy food chain. Timmon was avoiding service, something you wouldn't expect from a keeper of the law. And, of course, Neal was desperate because the hearing was Monday morning at ten-thirty, which meant I had to get Timmon served quickly or Monday morning would be a real bitch.

I walked into Neal's office at noon. Julietta was a spunky, good-looking Mexican girl who liked older guys. Having twenty years on her, I fit the profile, and, six years ago, she came on to me. Flattered by such attention, I told her I was trouble, she told me she liked trouble, I told her I was married, and she, being the good Catholic girl she was, told me it was a shame because if it wasn't for marriage and the holiness that came with it, she and I could get carnal in such a way that would send us both running to the confessional.

She gave me the subpoena and the three things I normally ask for: a work address, a home address, and a picture. Timmon was a young guy, in his early thirties, lean, a work-out-junky with black hair and a five o'clock shadow guys who *aren't* tough wear to make themselves *look* tough. If I had him pegged right, he'd puff up to twice his size then back down if things got physical.

Neal wanted me because the corporate guys couldn't get it done. You see, I am relentless. And I have a reputation for that. I will follow a guy into the shower if that's what it takes to get him served.

"Julietta," I said, "one of these days I'm going to tell Neal 'no' when he needs me. Then what?"

"You haven't told him 'no' yet," she said.

And she knew I was bullshitting because I needed the money, I *always* needed the money. Why? Because I was a little guy, I would always *be* a little guy, I knew my place in the world, I was a rabbit, not a lion, and lion's go where they want, when they want, and rabbits, well, they stay clear of lions.

I went straight over to Timmon's office, a big law firm that took up two floors at the top of a tall building with a sweet view of downtown. I walked through a pair of foyer-doors (a waste of good wood in my humble opinion) into a room with a receptionist, a scowl painted on her face that gave her every right to be lonely. She and I hit it off poorly, me being the type she wouldn't go near if she had a choice, her being the type who would have to settle for a guy like me.

I told her I wanted Gil Timmon. I had a subpoena, a *federal* subpoena, with the emphasis on Uncle Sam. She told me to take a seat, I did, while she picked up the phone. She kept it low so I couldn't hear then came back to me that Mr. Timmon was busy. She didn't know when he'd be free.

So, knowing that lawyers, like everybody else, go home at end of the day, I sat and I watched and I watched and I sat, a hard thing for me since patience doesn't come naturally. At five in the evening, the law firm of *Kuperman and Cody* emptied out.

"You'll have to leave now, sir," said my all-time-favorite receptionist, the one with the frown that didn't do her much good. She nodded at those foyer-doors that had disappointed me earlier.

"No Timmon?" I asked.

"Could be he left through another door. We're not a one-door law firm."

I scampered over to Timmon's house, on a Friday in rush-hour, where I found his place to be a spread on the West side. I parked at the curb, climbed steps up a small hill, then through an iron gate to a storm-door. Behind the glass was a front door which went very well with a big, expensive house.

I put in ten minutes of on-again, off-again knocking, then went back to my pickup where I sat for another couple of hours. The house stayed dark, no lights went on, nobody came or went. It was nine when I gave it up.

Next morning, I was back at Timmon's house at eight. I sat there until ten o'clock, nobody coming or going, everything looking dead like it did the night before. I had another paper to serve, a Mexican fella on the East side, one Ricardo Guzman, so I took a break from Timmon's house.

Guzman was an easy serve. I caught him in his garage lifting weights. There was a heavy-bag alongside a weight bench and barbells that reminded me of my set-up. Guzman was in top shape and the way he hit the bag while we talked told me he had a pretty good knuckle game. He and I got somewhat friendly once we connected over our workout routines. Him getting sued, he understood, had nothing personal to do with me.

I asked him if he did any roadwork. He said he didn't, that he kept it all weights and the heavy-bag which didn't surprise me. My experience, Mexican guys don't jog. It's all weight-work and punching on the heavy-bag. You want to find joggers, go back to the West side. The East side's got a culture all its own.

I grabbed a sandwich at a convenience store along with a bottle of water then went back to Timmon's house at 2:00. Timmon was avoiding service. Him being a lawyer, he knew the game and was no doubt combining a restful weekend away from home with ducking me.

At 11:00 p.m., I got tired of waiting and called Neal Green at his office. Neal works hard, long hours, weekends included. Neal's got a major-league work ethic so I knew he'd be waiting to hear from me.

"Neal, I been on this two days. Two long days. It ain't gonna happen."

"Augie, I need this guy's testimony. I don't have him, I'm sunk."

"Neal, he ain't coming home tonight. He's avoiding. I'll get him tomorrow. In one hour, it's tomorrow anyway."

Federal Rules of Civil Procedure don't make it clear you can serve a subpoena on Sundays. You serve a federal subpoena on a Sunday, it's open to interpretation. Doesn't say you can, doesn't say you can't. Some of my brethren process servers have no problem delivering such a service. Others, the careful ones, and the lawyers they deliver for, won't chance a federal subpoena served on Sunday. I am of the careful variety, and so is Neal.

"You know what that means, Neal."

"Yeah, Augie, I do."

"And?"

"Well, Augie, we have no choice, do we?"

"Not the way I see it."

"You think the subpoena will hold up, Augie?"

"You're the lawyer in this conversation, Neal. It's

your call. Way I see it, we got nothing to lose if we serve him tomorrow."

I drove home, showered, went to bed and slept sleepless. I got up in the dark, drank my coffee hot and black, then drove back to Timmon's house thinking maybe Hell was a place where you were tired all the time.

Timmon's house was like it was six hours earlier. If they came home late, they were snug in their beds, but I sort of doubted it. I've been at this a long time. I can smell if somebody's dodging service.

I parked along the curb, settled in, and watched the sun come up over Timmon's roof. I watched birds eat bugs. I watched wet grass turn dry. Ten minutes every hour I got out my truck and stretched. I took a pisser at a nearby gas station that had a toilet I wouldn't sit down on. Mixed in all that, I made my Christmas list early thinking I'd get Sandy some jewelry and Jack a meal at his favorite health-nut place.

At two in the afternoon, a gold Lexis SUV came toward me. The driver and I got a good look at each other when it slowed. It was Timmon. A woman sat in the front seat who I figured to be his wife. A couple of small kids were in the back seat. Timmon looked confused at first then gave me a "FUCK-YOU" stare once he put together what I was there for. The Lexis took a left into the driveway behind me then climbed the hill and disappeared around the corner of the house.

I gave it five minutes, and then went to the front door where I knocked hard and steady. A pissed-off Timmon would be better than no Timmon at all. It became apparent he wouldn't come to the door, and that his family was coached not to answer my knock, so I went back down to my car and called Julietta.

"He's holed up in his house," I said.

"What do you need from me?" she asked.

"Call their number. Tell them I'm down here, I'm not going away, and I'll beat on the door every thirty minutes if they don't answer. And Julietta, if you can, deliver that message to *Mrs.* Timmon."

I hung up and waited. I didn't know if Timmon's phone was listed or unlisted. A couple of minutes later Julietta called back.

"I got Mrs. Timmon," she said. "I think you'll be seeing Mr. Timmon any second now."

I looked at the driveway and saw Timmon coming down. He wore baggy, blue, basketball trunks, a white T-shirt that fit him snug, and jogging shoes. He came to the passenger side of the car. I rolled down the automatic window.

"Fuck you," he yelled. "You called my wife!"

I shrugged.

"Asshole! I don't have to be nice to you. I can say anything I want to you."

I shrugged.

"Give me the goddamn paper," he yelled.

"You come around here," I said.

I got out the truck and shut the door as he came around the backside. He was my height. Like Guzman, I hit the heavy-bag regularly. I can throw up to fifty punches a minute. I work that bag four times a week, an hour at a time. Timmon, with that silly five o'clock shadow that would get him bitch-slapped on the East side, didn't scare me. I've been shot at, and chased by a pit bull. Timmon took the subpoena and walked off.

I called Julietta and told her to expect my bill. I told her Neal was looking at two-hundred dollars and I made no guarantee Timmon would show. I put the paper in his hand. I did my work.

I came home to a note from Sandy that said to call Jack. So, Jack and I had a brief phone-chat about things in general and did some catching up. Jack told me things were going so well it scared him, which is the mindset that says it all about the Spiveys.

Jack brought up that our Uncle Rex passed away. Rex was our old man's oldest brother. In my view, Rex was a war hero who flew under the radar and who didn't get medals or his picture in a magazine. But he fought the Nazis in Europe, came home worried and sick, got his health back, then built a life around his family and friends and made everybody better for it.

I didn't fight in any wars. My pals were all Viet Nam guys, but I didn't serve. Sometimes I regret that, because maybe if you go to war you come back with a different perspective, you have an edge, a bigger point of view that tells you such things as football games on Saturday or arguments with your wife aren't any big thing. But I've seen death early, and how it marches, and that's enough war for me.

17

THE SAME DAMN DREAM

I still say my prayers. Every morning I toss out a couple of Hail Marys for my family and friends and world peace. I've got no faith in world peace, but what's one more prayer?

I took a call at breakfast that had me almost lose my pancakes. When I was done, I hung up the phone and Sandy asked me what it was that caused me such agitation.

"That was Sister Mary Clooney, my old principal. Go figure."

It was the good sisters of the Holy Spirit who taught me right from wrong and all about this prayer thing I've got for a habit that won't go away. Every now and then, when I think about a walk on the dark side, one of those nuns pops into my head and gives me a look that says it's my soul we're talking about here.

I got in my Toyota pickup and drove cross-town. My old school sits in a neighborhood that used to be white but isn't white any more. School was in session, kids (Asians, Mexicans, and a couple of white kids) were playing where I used to play. Boys were all dressed in khaki pants and white shirts with collars. The girls were wearing jumpers with the white blouses, the kind my mother ordered for my sisters out the Catholic catalogue. It took me back to the last time I felt safe.

I walked in the principal's office. It had the same desk, same walls, same smell, and Sister Mary Clooney behind that desk. She wasn't the young Irish girl who smacked our bodies around to save our souls. She was older, much older, forty years older. Like a time-machine, it put me back in grade number eight. She still had her magic.

"Hello, August," she said. "Life has been good to you, I hope."

And life had been good. Good enough that I couldn't complain. Sure, it had its ups and downs. I didn't keep score, no point in that. But I was alive, ate good, and slept soundly on rare occasions. I had my own occupation, one that made me walk tall and proud. I had a wife who understood me, and a couple of things left to believe in.

"Yeah," I said," and thanks for asking."

Then she and I took a walk around the old school. Holy Rosary hadn't changed. It still had that tired look; an asphalt-blacktop quadrangle surrounded by a yellow-brick building with doors that opened directly to the outside.

"Frank, you remember August Spivey, don't you?"

Frank Cantu was janitor when I came through. Bent over, muscled up, he had three lips: two on top, one on the bottom. The story went he got his upper lip torn in half boxing down in Mexico. Got it stitched up by some local-yokel who called himself a doctor. Frank was no "contenda." But I guess he was one hell of a janitor.

"No," he mumbled.

So, Sister Mary Clooney, with Frank Cantu nodding, and me listening, took us over to the gym, a building that had been our old church, that once housed God, but was now four walls of dust and sweat.

"We were so close to refurbishing this building, August. Come in for a minute."

And sure enough, things were taking shape. Those old, inside walls had been painted, there were grandstands, and a gym floor that looked recent enough to call new. We stepped back outside.

"Our plan was to add on new siding. The old exterior was simply rotten. The mildew won the battle of time. You remember, August, how Frank was always scrubbing down this building?"

"No," I said, then felt like a prick because I did remember Frank climbing those walls like a big bug, had a brush in one hand, a bucket in the other. Back breaking work only a guy made out of steel could do.

"August, to be succinct, someone stole our siding two nights ago." She sighed. "Who would do something so cowardly to these poor children?"

For the first time, Sister Mary Clooney took a minute, walked away, and had herself a cry. Frank and I waited patiently, one minute, maybe two. We let Clooney pull herself together. She came back red-eyed but ready to take on the world.

"You call the police?" I asked.

"Yes, they took information, but they as much as said they had bigger things to worry about." She looked around the neighborhood that surrounded the school. "It's gotten quite rough around here."

"So, insurance?" I asked.

"None, I'm afraid. We're poor. You know that. Five years of saving pennies and nickels. Paper drives, cake sales. These children gave so much toward this. Oh my!"

Worried I was she might go teary on me again, but she took a nun-pill and turned back into Mother Superior.

"August, I need you. Your old school needs you. These children need you."

"Need me for what?"

"To find that siding."

Then it hit me like (I imagined) the punch that gave Frank three lips instead of two. She knew I was a private eye. I hadn't said a word about what I did. But she *knew*.

She might've heard it through the nun-grapevine. Might've found me in a phone book and my name rang a bell with her. One thing was sure: she was desperate and August Spivey was her last card.

"All of these wonderful children and I have been praying to God on this August. Haven't we, Frank?"

"Yeth."

"You really think God's going to fix this?" I asked.

"Yes, I do, August. He sent you."

She and Frank walked back to the school. This was Clooney's life, her reason for getting up in the morning: to save souls, and make this lousy stay on planet-earth a little better for some of those who couldn't catch a break no matter how hard they tried. I left things in a state of non-commitment, but I knew it was on me to find that siding. If I didn't come through, I'd have to look Clooney in the eye, and Frank in the lip, and tell myself I failed.

If Clooney's problem wasn't big enough, I still had to make a living. You see, August Spivey *does live* on bread alone. I had a paper to serve for Neal Green and I needed it done by end of business tomorrow. I'd had it near a week but its intended recipient, a bartender name of Huey Buell, was doing a fine job of avoiding me. I knew where he worked, which should've made the service easy, but my two visits there produced no Huey. And he had no address since his eviction from an apartment a month ago. I could only figure he was doing what I would do: lay low and sleep on a buddy's couch.

I phoned Neal Green on my cell to give him an update. Neal practices law by screaming over the phone. Someday, the screaming will stop, along with eating, and breathing, and all the other things we-the-living do. Until then, Neal and I get through things the hard way.

"Goddamn, you haven't served that paper yet? What the fuck am I paying you for? I WANT THAT PAPER SERVED NOW!"

"Okay Neal," I said, "let's start with me telling you to get fucked. Normally, I wouldn't say that to anybody who I'm delivering paper for, but I don't work for you, we do business together. And if you don't want to do business with me, then great, because I'm getting fed up with you hiring some stuffed-shirt, TV-ad, yellow pages, drugstore private eye firm with some glitzy corporate look to do what I can do better than them any day of the week, and then you have the balls to come back to me when they can't get it done and treat me like I'm your little bitch. Have I ever let you down? Neal, I'm talking to you!"

"No, you've never let me down."

"Have I ever not put paper directly into a guy's hands?"

"No."

"So shut the fuck up or you and me are done. I DON'T NEED YOU. You will have your paper served no later than tomorrow night which, by the way, is the time you told me you needed it served. Are we clear, or should I make a paper airplane out of your lawsuit?"

"You'll have it served by tomorrow?" asked Green.

"Yes, by five."

"OK, then."

He hung up like he was the guy calling the shots but I had it on him and we both knew it.

I went back to discovering where the hell the siding went. Normally, I limit myself to undercover work in bars and restaurants, and delivering civil process for litigators like Neal Green. The kind of fieldwork needed here was the door-to-door type that gets people suspicious or mad. And you don't make any money. See, a guy hires you, maybe he's had his car stolen, he wants you to find it. So you go around asking if anybody saw any shady-types hanging around that car. The guy who hires you wants to get the biggest bang for his buck, right? So he tries to low-ball you, maybe authorizes you an hour or two to get the information you need to find his car. Well, that won't do. You need at least five or six hours minimum. If he gives you that much time or more, you better come back with something substantial. You do the work, you ask the questions, and nothing comes of it because your average Joe Schmo isn't paying attention to the world going on around him, and if he did see something he doesn't want to get involved. All that leads to you not getting paid because the man who hired you thinks he's paying for nothing. What are you going to do? Sue him? You get my point?

I knocked on a couple of doors across the street from the school and got no answer. One house had a Mexican guy out in front mowing his yard. He took a minute to visit with me but saw nothing that looked funny at the school. The siding got stolen over-night, so, unless he or someone else was up late, I figured nothing helpful was coming from the neighbors. I'd come back later.

I drove to a neighborhood grocery store run by the Tino family. Mr. and Mrs. Tino opened the store fifty years ago. Mr. Tino was dead and Mrs. Tino lived with her daughter, Leslie. Mr. Tino was always good about spotting in his kids where their talents were then helping them go in that direction. There are six Tino kids, five boys and one girl. Two of the boys, Eddie and Vic are lawyers. Leslie teaches school, last I heard. Tommy, Stevie and Fabian run the grocery store.

Fabian and I have been friends since we were kids at Holy Rosary. When we were in the second grade, Fabian came down with a case of polio in his right foot that made him limp. Mr. Tino, being the parent he was, pushed Fabian into the martial arts because it was clear Fabian was losing his confidence. He wasn't talking to girls. He wasn't doing well in school. Experience has taught me that inferiority can make you very quiet or very loud. Some guys want to be noticed, some guys want to hide. In Fabian's case, he wanted to hide.

Martial arts was the best thing that could've happened to Fabian. He's in full possession of himself, but if he gets pushed too far, he can go crazy and unmerciful on you. I saw him beat the shit out of a guy one night. We were in a bar when some drunk started badgering Fabian and wouldn't let up. When Fabian was done, the prick crawled out the bar on his hands and knees, a lot of blood and teeth left on the floor. Fabian walks soft and carries a very big stick. I'd rather step barefoot on a rattle snake than piss him off.

I told Fabian what happened with the siding. I requested that if he or anybody who worked in the store even *heard* the word "siding" could they give me a call? In my view, whoever took the siding would want to dump it fast. *Tino's* grocery had always been one of those places you could pick up neighborhood chatter. Somebody dies, somebody's princess gets knocked-up, somebody has an affair, you heard about it first in *Tino's* grocery.

It didn't surprise me that Fabian was on board with helping me track down the siding. He had a special place in his heart for Holy Rosary. One day, he worried, the school would run out of money and shut down. Knock on wood, so far no priest, who had come through Holy Rosary, had gotten funny with an altar boy.

I took a late lunch at Slippey's, a place I'd never been in. It was pushing three o'clock and I was hungry. I hadn't had a real meal since the night before. I ordered a plate of barbecued chicken smothered in sauce and caramelized onions. On the side, I had a small hill of coleslaw and bowl of beans that would have me farting into the next life. I chased it with a *Miller High Life* so cold my nuts chattered. I made a note to self that Slippey's was my kind of place.

I made a quick stop at the *Firefly,* the bar where Huey Buell worked. The *Firefly* is a rough place to drink, full of construction workers blowing off steam during happy-hour and on football weekends. It's a place an average schmo like me can go in and come out feeling smart.

Buell wasn't there and I was starting to sweat another face-off with Neal Green. The idea of Neal having the upper fist on me got me started on my daily heartburn. I'd tried twice before at the *Firefly* and had enough with this visit to put in for substitute service. But I like proving myself to Neal, especially when he's being a prick. My guess was that by now Buell knew I was on to where he worked and with the other bartender playing dumb and a truckload of siding somewhere in a city of several million human beings, I wrote the day off as a loss.

Sandy was put out with me at dinner when I wouldn't sit down to a full meal. I nibbled here and there on her roast and mashed potatoes. The chicken in my tummy wasn't in a sharing mood.

After dinner Sandy and I went to work painting the living-room walls and ceiling. She hit the detail stuff, I handled the roller. I'm not a workaholic. But the older I get, the more I need to keep busy. I'm getting where I can't sit still for too long.

We had a bowl of peach ice cream, and then went to bed about ten. The painting left me tired enough to drop off into sleep. Next thing I knew, Sean Rust and I were at Holy

Rosary, standing in front of a big, green Nazi swastika that he and I painted on the yellow-brick wall next to the boy's crapper. He and I didn't think about what it meant. We didn't think how many people it fucked up. We saw it on TV, maybe in a war movie. Thought it was cool. It had straight lines. It had a design to it and people saluting it. We drew it. We knew right away we were in trouble. We made a pact to never talk about it again. The next day, Sister Clooney got on the school intercom. She said she wanted the boys who did it to step up, to show they were repentant. And when we didn't come forward, she wouldn't take it down. She'd keep it there forever to let those who did it know how stained-up their souls were. Forty years ago! Forty years ago! Still on that wall– still on that wall– STILL ON THAT WALL!

"What wall?" asked Sandy. I woke up to her shaking me sturdy.

"Goddamn," I said. "She knew it was us who did it."

"Who knew who did what?"

"She's expecting me to set things right."

"Set what things right, Augie?"

After my dream, I slept feverishly. I told Sandy it could wait. Next morning, I showered cold and drank a cup of black coffee to get my daytime rhythm back. Once I was up and around, dealing in the world of priority, I took Neal Green's paper over Sister Mary Clooney's siding. It comes to choices, a man's got to take care of business or he won't eat. I'd need a break to find that siding and I don't believe much in luck or divine intervention.

Unexpectedly, I got a phone call.

"Augie, there's a guy in my store as we speak talking on his cell phone. The word *siding* came up several times in his conversation."

It was Fabian Tino just about the time I was heading off to the *Firefly* in my dimming hopes of serving Huey Buell.

"You think he'll be there a while?" I asked.

"Don't know," said Fabian.

"He leaves," I said, "get his plates."

I bolted for *Tino's* grocery. Traffic was heavy. Rush-hour clogged things up. Patience isn't one of my strengths. I wasn't afraid to use my horn.

I pulled into the parking lot where Fabian told me I missed the guy by ten minutes. Fabian got his plates and his description. He was tall and thin. A yellow man. An Asian with a pony tail. He drove a Tundra.

I thanked Fabian and told him the two of us needed to break bread in the near future. I called Sandy who ran the plates and gave me the owner's address. Twenty minutes later I was parked on a street eyeballing a Tundra.

A guy came out of a house that looked rental-variety. Like the houses around it, the yard wasn't kept top-notch. It needed a lake dropped on it and a serious dose of green-thumb. The description of the guy fit: Asian with a pony tail. He backed the Tundra out of the driveway and went right past me. I laid back then followed him out of his neighborhood onto the freeway. It was tough, but I kept him in sight.

Twenty miles later the Tundra pulled onto a feeder road that connected with a rural route. I knew the area. I'd spent plenty of time out there. He took the route for another five miles and then hung a right into a country subdivision made up of tiny lots carved out of land some farmer sold for his retirement. I got a bad feeling.

He took one more left turn and I knew things weren't going to end good. He pulled onto a driveway that had a black pickup truck I knew all too well. I stayed back, watching things unwind. He got out of his Tundra, then walked along the driveway where he disappeared. I waited on calling the cops. I let a few more minutes go by, then walked along the same driveway into the backyard.

A pallet of siding sat behind a detached garage. Two men stood next to it. One was the Asian, the other was ….

"Augie, what the hell are you doing here?"

"Looking for siding, Sean."

Sean Rust walked up to me and offered a hand I didn't take.

"What kind of siding?" asked Sean, making bad with a joke.

"The stolen kind that belongs to a nun and a bunch of poor kids."

Sean and I had a tense moment, one waiting for the other to talk. The Asian looked genuinely surprised. That told me he didn't know what was going on.

"Ok, Augie, so now what?" asked Sean, who finally broke silence.

"I don't know what the hell this is about," said the Asian. "I got word from a source I thought was legit that this stuff was for sale. I got nothing to do with it if it's hot."

"Oh," I said, "it's hot."

"You a cop?" asked the Asian.

"No, and I can't keep you here," I said.

"He's fresh to this," said Sean. "He don't know anything about it."

The Asian spent no time getting lost. It left me and Sean Rust with a dilemma. I don't rat out a pal without some serious reflection.

"We're giving it back, Augie," said a familiar voice that came from behind. It was Sean's wife, Patty. She, Sean and I went back a very long way. "We're out of money," she said. "You ever been out of money, Augie?"

And truth be known, Patty caught me with my dick in my hand. She and Sean more than once loaned me and Sandy money when we needed it.

"You really taking it back, or is this bullshit?" I asked.

"Yeah, I'm really taking it back and this ain't bullshit."

"So, why was that guy just here?"

"He came unsolicited. Sent here by a third party. I already made my mind up to give it back before he got here. He walked up on me while I was here in the yard."

"That's right," said Patty. "Sean's not lying."

I didn't ask who Sean's broker on this deal was. Might've been somebody else I knew. This was already too much.

"So, what you up against?" I asked.

"Mortgage, groceries, about a thousand bucks this month and next."

Sean was a construction worker who hadn't driven a nail in weeks. I told him and Patty that if he took the siding back, I'd cover his costs for two months. Sandy would be on board. She and Patty were close.

"You take it back, the church will probably help you out a little," I said.

"What you think Clooney will do?" asked Sean. "You think she'll call the cops?"

"No, she'll be disappointed. She'll think she fucked up her calling. Might push you toward the confessional, but she's a forgiver. I would steer clear of Frank Cantu, if I were you."

Sean and I shook on it. Patty, normally tougher than nails, got a little teary. Before I left I asked what caused the change of heart. Patty was always Sean's angel-voice so I figured it was her who pushed for the right thing.

"Tell him, Sean," said Patty.

"I had a dream was you and me standing in front of that green thing we drew on the wall. You remember that?"

"I do."

"It wouldn't go away. I kept having it. It wouldn't go away."

It was three o'clock when I rolled up on the *Firefly*. I had Buell's plates and I spotted his car, a white 2006 Geo Prism, parked in the alley behind the bar. I know where people like to hide their cars.

I walked in and sat at the bar. Happy-hour was beginning to take shape. There was one guy working the bar. He and I had been round and round on Buell three times by now and I was in no mood to bullshit. Being a former bartender, I knew there was no way one bartender worked happy hour on Friday by himself.

A pair of rednecks were sitting at a table to my right. They were younger than me and appeared to be having fun at my expense. One was blowing kisses at me, the other having a good laugh.

"You know who I am and why I'm here, right?"

"Yeah, and he ain't here," said the bartender.

"Oh, but he is," I said. "His car's out back." I nodded at a door that sat at the end of the bar. "Tell Buell I'm sitting here and drinking until *last call* if I have to. He ain't making any money tonight if he stays behind that door."

The bartender walked to the door and opened it.

"Huey, he ain't leaving."

Buell came out and I served him as easy as that.

"Why'd you make this so hard?" I asked

"I dunno," said Buell.

I gave a quick glance to the two rednecks who continued to make disrespectful gestures my way.

"You know those two?" I asked Buell.

"Yeah, that's Doug and Bobby."

"They badasses? " I asked.

"Depends," said Buell.

I pulled twenty bucks from my wallet.

"When I signal you, send over three *Blue Ribbon* beers. Keep the change. And here's ten bucks more since I hate being the bearer of your bad news."

I strolled over to Doug and Bobby's table where I sat down without invitation. The rednecks who I know think beer is blood. I've seen rednecks drink *Blue Ribbon* at funerals.

"You boys are either flirting with me or fucking with me. Which is it?"

"Well, we ain't flirting," said Doug. They were both big, but Doug came across real fast as the guy who made the decisions.

"*Well,* here's my deal. I can buy us a round of beers, or we can go out in the parking lot and I don't care how the fuck it turns out."

"I do believe this fine gentleman has just bought us our next beer. What say you to that, Bobby?" asked Doug.

Bobby nodded. I waived Buell over with the *Blue Ribbons*. Doug, Bobby and I had a nice visit about a few things we had in common.

I called Neal Green's office, said I was on the way with Buell's proof of service. I rolled into traffic with Led Zepplin blaring away on the radio. I like Rock n' Roll. Good Rock n' Roll. The kind that goes with celebrating.

18

OLD SCHOOL

Prince Tomanet needed a favor. He and I met during my bartending period, me as a mixologist, him as a teenage kid who somehow conned his way into a bouncing job. We were pals, and in my world, pals take care of pals.

Prince made his living throwing people out of bars. He was built for it: big, strong, agile. But he wanted out of the bouncer's world. Lifestyle drove his decision; booze, cocaine, nameless sex partners, fun for a while, were wearing out his twenty-eight-year-old body.

Prince was a smart guy. He came from a family loaded up with brains. His parents were college professors, his brother a downtown lawyer. People told me Prince had an IQ that put him in a group of special people.

But you couldn't tell him *anything*. He was jack-ass stubborn and weak on the self-discipline. My brother Jack says a guy who can't control his appetites is inviting failure. Prince, for some crazy reason, looked up to me. Such respect doesn't often come my way.

Prince wanted into the lawsuit-paper business. He was naive, thinking it would be easy. Sometimes *it is*. You have an address, you take a drive, you time it right, you catch your boy just about the time he's getting home from a long day of bread-winning. If he's naturally polite or a professional who separates business from the personal, you hand him that lawsuit-paper, wish him only the best, and move on. I once served a board of directors, twelve of them, sitting around a big, wooden table like Christ and his supper guests. I made seven-hundred bucks in five minutes. Smoothest money I've ever earned.

But it's not always that easy. When it's hard, it's real hard. *Dangerous* hard. And *crazy* at times. I've been physically threatened; had guns pointed at me. I once served paper on a woman who came to the front door naked. This is not a job for a weak stomach or thin skin. It's a profession for people who don't fit in. It's for outsiders. It's not normal. *It takes balls.*

That, by the way, is why I'm the best. Anybody can drive by a guy's house, leave a petition tagged to the front door, then swear in an affidavit he couldn't deliver it personally. I put it in their hand. That's foolproof. You put me on a witness stand, ask me if I served paper on a guy in the legally correct way, I'll look you dead in the eye. I get the jobs the other guys can't do. In lawyer circles, I'm known for that.

Prince took on a paper from Jimmy Short, a lawyer who I knew personally, had done work for, and who acted like his piss was holy water. Prince had no business holding himself out as an experienced process server. He called me, asking for advice. I agreed, but had my conditions.

"Here's the deal," I said, "I help you get this paper served, you shut up and do what I tell you. I'm Yoda, you're Luke Skywalker. We clear?"

The big lunk nodded. Before we hit the road, we took a minute to hash out some strategy. I'm *old school.* You learn from me, you learn things right. Help a guy catch a fish, he gets to eat today. Help a guy *learn how to fish,* odds are he won't go hungry the rest of his life.

I took the petition from Prince. The lawsuit was styled *William Sanchez v. Carl Bumpas,* filed in the tenth-district court.

"When did you get this?" I asked.

"Yesterday, at noon."

"And you have until end of day, tomorrow, to get this served?"

"That's right," said Prince.

"So, in all, they gave you fifty hours, give or take?"

"Right again."

I figured out what was going on. Jimmy took on the client and, seeing the statute of limitations was about to run out on his client's lawsuit, had to get the suit filed. Once he made that timeline, he set the court date *before* he got the paper served. He should have waited *until* the paper got served to set the court date. Now, the court date was getting close and Jimmy, like most solo practitioners who take on more than they can handle, and who put the cart in front of the horse, was under pressure which puts the process server under pressure *if* the server lets himself get pushed around.

"OK, first things first," I said. "This is a rush. Short is feeling some heat. When a lawyer is under the gun, remember, he needs you more than you need him. You drive the deal. Don't let him drive you. When I get a rush-job like this, I make them guarantee me three hours up front. That's $150.00. If I get the party served fast, it's quick money. If it takes a while, like this is shaping up to be, I still get my expenses covered and usually make a little money. How much did you charge for this?"

"Forty dollars, " said Prince.

"You see how chasing around like this makes you no money?" I asked.

"I do," he answered.

The address Short's office gave Prince said 6210 Walnut Street which sat in a subdivision not far off.

"A couple of thoughts," I said. "See that return section at the bottom of the petition?"

"Yeah."

"Fill it out as much as you can before you serve your boy. You want to spend minimal time with somebody who probably is not going to like you. All you want left is the space for your initials and the date. You can plug that stuff in when you get back in your car. That way, you're out of there quick. You mess around too long on a man's porch, and he's got dogs, he might put them on you. Prince, this is serious business."

I pointed to the address that was given to Prince.

"Tell me what went wrong here."

"I went out there. I couldn't find the address."

"No *6210* or no *Walnut Street*?"

"No *6210.*"

We took off driving for *Walnut Street,* about fifteen minutes away. Prince complained he'd been out there, going back was a waste of time.

"When it comes to this business, who's the Jedi warrior in this car?"

"You are," he answered.

"Last time I remind you, OK?"

"Yeah."

"OK?" I repeated.

"Yes, OK, I got it."

We pulled on to *Walnut Street;* twenty houses, some new, some partially built, all of them the kind Theodore Cleaver could feel warm and safe in.

"You see what I mean?" asked Prince.

"Yeah," I agreed.

None of the addresses came close. *Walnut Street* was a long way from being finished. Someday a developer would smile ear to ear but right now it was part of a subdivision going up one house at a time.

"What do we do?" asked Prince.

"You tell me," I coaxed.

172

"I guess we knock on doors," he said.

"Did it cross your mind," I offered, "that Short's office made a mistake?"

Prince shrugged.

"Call them," I said.

He opened his cell phone and dialed.

"What do I say?"

"Don't ask them if they made a mistake. You tell them you're out here with a bad address. Put it on them to fix it. Tell them you need it *now*, not in a little while. We can't wait on a phone call."

I listened while Prince went back and forth with Jimmy Short's paralegal. In a corporate outfit, the paralegals are on the ball. If they get things wrong, it could cost them their job. A small firm can be different, especially if it's a one-man operation. The girl might be sleeping with the boss. If she has an attitude, she can get away with it if her and the boss are cozy. I knew Jimmy Short well enough to think he could be nailing Sheila Gould. Below the neck, Sheila was a *ten*, above it, I doubt she could count that high.

"Tell her to get the file and verify the address," I whispered, "and say it like you mean it."

Prince did what I told him. We waited while Sheila went for the file.

"She's pissed off," Prince said.

"So am I," I answered, "and you should be by now."

Prince went back to talking with Sheila.

"She says there's no address in the file."

"Ask her if she remembers what other files she was working on at the time."

"She says she can't remember," said Prince.

"Ask her how bad her boss wants this paper

served," I responded.

We waited.

"That paper doesn't get served," I said, "she'll blame it on you."

Prince winked at me a few seconds later.

"Oh, wrong file? You got *6210 Walnut Street* out of another file?" he asked into the phone.

"Ask her if she's got anything on Bumpas," I suggested.

"You got anything on Bumpas?" he asked her.

"Ask her to spell his name," I said.

Prince asked, then said aloud, *"B-U-M-P-A-S."*

"Tell her to find Bumpas's address and call you back asap," I said.

He delivered the message then hung up.

"I thought you said we couldn't wait on her to call back?" questioned Prince.

"I did that to mess up her afternoon," I answered.

I took out my cell phone, and then phoned *INFORMATION.* I got two hits for Carl Bumpas: one with a number and address, the other unlisted. I had no time to fool with Sheila. I called Sandy and had her do a quick address check on Bumpas. The number we got from Ma Bell and what Sandy dug up were the same.

Thirty minutes later we rolled up a long, cement driveway far out in the country. The house had money written all over it and sat on a chunk of good-looking green land with a front yard that had what people call *"curb appeal."*

I always look for dogs. I can't emphasize that enough. If a rich guy owns a dog, it might be a *Fi-Fi* or a *Fido.* You talk nice to a dog like that, they wag their tale and slobber on you. Rich people have burglar bars and high-tech stuff that keeps the bad boys out of their house.

The East side is different. You walk into a poor-man's yard, you're probably going to meet a pit bull or a doberman. On the East side, they keep their security on a chain.

"Prince," I asked, "you ever run into any dogs?"

"Not yet," he answered.

"You ever do, here's a little trick I learned."

I honked my horn three times, then took out my keys and shook them. No dogs came running.

"This'll get them out from wherever they are," I instructed. "Always check out the dogs, first thing. If there's a dog on a chain, you want to make sure that chain doesn't stretch far enough that he can get at you. If you see a chain, and you can get at it with your car, roll your front wheels over it. That should take the slack out of the chain. It won't hurt the dog. He'll be madder than hell that you have him short-chained, but it'll keep your legs attached to your body and, God help you, that thing that swings between them."

The front door to the house opened. A big guy wearing a light-blue robe came walking out to the car. He looked about forty, soft, happy like he ate good, slept good, and had plenty of good luck.

"I'm looking for Carl Bumpas," I stated.

I eye-balled his look. It was level. If a guy's lying to me, I can tell.

"Do you mind if I ask what you want?" he asked.

"I have his wallet," I lied. "My name's August Spivey."

"And you have *my* address?"

"Yeah," I said, "it's in the wallet."

I watched his hand. It was steady as a board. You tell a guy you have his wallet, he usually makes some sort of move to his pocket. Power of suggestion is a useful thing.

We backed out of the driveway then stopped a couple of hundred feet down the road.

"That might have been our guy," said Prince.

"It wasn't," I answered.

"What if he asked to see the wallet you said you had?"

"He didn't."

"How could you be sure he wouldn't have?"

"I wasn't. I rolled the dice he'd have his wallet with him. In this business, you need to read people."

"And you could tell by reading that guy he wasn't Bumpas?"

"I could tell by reading the guy he wasn't *our* Carl Bumpas."

"That's a little thin, don't you think, Augie? We got it from the phone book. Your own wife verified the name."

"It's not our guy, Prince. You'll see."

Things got a little quiet in the car. Prince could be sullen. I'm normally not the smartest guy in the room, but I respect experience. I reminded Prince that it never hurts to get a picture of the guy you're tracking. You need to ask the paralegal who gives you the paper. Many a time it's in the file and they just forget. I also gave him a look that said he picked the wrong day to mess with August Spivey's patience.

"Where we going now?" he asked.

"The post office," I answered.

We pulled up on a post office that sat between a pair of small buildings at an intersection of two asphalt roads.

"We need an address," I said to a female postal clerk who looked no more than twenty years old.

"Might I ask why?" she said.

"We need to deliver civil process on a guy being sued."

I leaned over the counter and whispered confidentially, "It's time-sensitive."

Nowadays, if you want an unlisted address, you fill out a form. Out in the rural areas, sometimes you have to make nice with the postal workers and hope they're not having a bad day.

"I'm really not supposed to do this," she said.

"If it can get you in trouble, don't do it," I sympathized.

She looked at Prince. Big as he was, he wasn't a bad-looking fella. He had thick black hair and a scar that went down the left side of his face, compliments of a broken beer bottle. I've met women who admitted to getting worked up over stitch-work on a man. A guy can be a *Grade A* scumbag, but if he wears a face-zipper he won't go lonely.

"Just this once," she said.

I nodded agreeably. "I doubt we'll be back through here again."

I gave her a piece of paper that had written on it Carl Bumpas's name. A minute later she came back with the unlisted address.

We got in the car and started driving. I was feeling the chase. We were smack-dab in hillbilly country; small, wooden houses, some neat, some run-down, set back in the woods.

"There," pointed Prince.

I hit my brakes then backed up fifty feet or so. I parked the car on the road facing the direction I wanted to leave. The first Bumpas address we stopped at had a long driveway that made it hard to run from trouble. You always want your car out on the road, away from buildings if you can manage it, pointed for a fast, smooth getaway.

I rolled down my window, shook my keys. The house was neat, well-built, with a freshly painted, white picket-fence around a clean, plain yard. A pickup was parked in the driveway. I looked in the pickup's front window as we walked past it.

"We have our boy," I said.

"More instinct?" asked Prince. He was pushing his luck with the tone.

"What's it say right there?" I asked. I pointed to the petition Prince had in his hand.

"It says Bumpas breached his contract with Sanchez. It says Bumpas agreed to put a swimming pool in Sanchez's back yard. It says Sanchez wants his pool or a whole bunch of money."

"What's that tell you about Bumpas?" I asked.

"It tells me owns a pool company," said Prince.

"Yeah," I agreed, "and that he probably digs those pools."

I nodded inside the pickup. It had four rolls of contractor's plans sitting on the front seat. A guy's car or driveway can tell you a lot. You see a ball glove or a football in the car, odds are the guy might be a pretty good athlete. If the car's messy with junk, it tells me he might be living alone. Few women put up with a dirty car. If there's a baby carrier in the front seat, he's a family man. How well you read a driveway and the car or truck that sits on it goes a long way in this business.

"Ok, Prince," I said, "back at that first address, that guy who you thought was the right Carl Bumpas, did you get a look at his hands?"

"No, I didn't," he answered.

"Well, I did. They were manicured. Would've made Liberace envious. The guy didn't hammer nails for a living. *This* Carl Bumpas puts in swimming pools."

We knocked on the front door. The thought occurred to me that both Bumpases might be family. I've seen cousins named after the same grandparent. It wouldn't help if Bumpas Number One had put in a call to his cousin, Bumpas Number Two. I kept my eye on a picture window to the right. You see a blind or a curtain move, just a little, you know you're being watched. After a couple of knocks, no one came to the door. I walked back to the pickup and felt its engine hood. It was warm.

"Come on," I said.

We jumped down from the porch and walked about thirty feet to a corner of the house. We took a right turn and walked another thirty or forty feet. We took one more right turn into the back yard where we ran smack-dab into a guy coming around the corner.

"Carl Bumpas?" I asked.

"Yeah," he said. "Who are you?"

His eyes narrowed. He looked stink-eyed at me, but he knew he was served.

"The jerk complained from the second my crew put shovel to ground. I couldn't do anything right by him. I oughta be suing *him*. It's backwards."

Several weeks went unnoticed. You get older, time scoots by on you. It's easy to lose track. I delivered my share of lawsuit-paper, some of it easy, some of it hard. I did some undercover work for a chain of restaurants. The chief operating officer and I hit it off good seven or eight years ago. He uses me when he knows his corporate people are coming in to check on his wait staff and bartenders. I don't do my work with the intention of getting anybody fired. It kills me if I hear a boy gets let go on account of my reports. But my duty is to my client. I catch anybody putting cash into his pocket instead of the register, or breaking house rules about dress code or attitude, it shows up in my report.

I didn't hear a word from Prince Tomanet. I stopped in one day to Jimmy Short's office. I thought I could pick up some lawsuit-paper as long as I wasn't taking work from Prince. Ours' is a business of survival, dog-eat-dog, but I don't steal bread from a pal. My code.

Jimmy was snotty as usual. Sheila had that pouty look which told me she could work a man with her moods. The both of them hadn't heard from Prince in a while.

Jimmy had no paper for me. Before I left I told him and Sheila not to forget me. I followed my visit with a phone call to Prince.

"Augie, I'm back to bouncing," he said.

"Why's that?" I asked.

"I got tired of lawyers."

I left bartending because *I got tired* of smokey rooms and loud drunks. And I didn't want people calling me *"Pops"* when I was fifty. A year ago I heard Prince Tomanet was dead. Heart attack. Too much cocaine. All that high IQ gone. One thing I've learned, in life there's a lot of waste.

19

A CAR CAPER

When the phone rings, I get edgy. When the phone rings it generally means work, and work means opportunity. You'd think I'd be excited, right? But I'm not. The first thing that crosses my mind when the phone rings is whether I'll be up to the job. Whether it will be dangerous. Whether I'll have to get down and dirty. Or whether I'll get shot at or beaten up. All of that stuff crosses my mind when the phone rings.

And I don't sleep. No matter what I do: cold showers, bedtime reading, shutting the TV off early in the evening, eyeshades, blackout curtains, none of it works. Jack tells me we have over-sensitive amygdalas. Leave it to Jack to come up with something like that. Before Jack informed me, I'd never heard of the word. Jack says it's a little knot of tissue that sits in the brain and lets you know when its fight or flight time. He says mine, and sometime his, won't shut off. That's a bad thing.

Our mother, I figure, had a nervous amygdala. She never slept. I'd be lying in bed, looking into our dark living room across the hall, watching her sit by herself at the end of the day, winding down from the five of us and our old man who was a drinker. I guess I come from a family with screaming amygdalas. Oh yes, when the phone rings, I get edgy.

The phone rang on a day in October. I was sitting at my desk, putting together my monthly invoice. I'd earned a bit less than a grand. I needed more. My budget calls for two-grand a month. That's my break-even. I can run my home office, take care of my car, cover my field expenses, and give Sandy a couple of hundred dollars when I pull in two "Gs" a month.

Mike Buck was on the phone. As lawyers go, Mike's a pleasure to work with. He's a "people" guy. He spends time on the phone with you making sure of the details. Compared to Neal Green or Gretchen Mueller, he's Saint Francis of Assisi. If all lawyers were like Mike Buck, that amygdala thing would shut up.

"Augie, I got a client who wants her car back."

"What kind of car?"

"A 2014 Corvette. Brand new. Less than ten thousand miles."

"I'd want it back, too," I said.

"Augie, I'll be brief. The particulars are my client's and my problem. What I need from you is the service of a TRO on the guy who has the car. We think he's getting ready to do something with it. My client gave the bad-guy possession of the car so it could be sold. It's been six months and the car hasn't sold, my client can't get her car back, and the bad-guy won't answer his phone."

I knew how extreme TROs were. What a pain in the ass they could be. But Mike had helped me when I needed back in the game, we'd been doing business for a long time, and he'd told me more than once that I was his "go-to" guy when the chips were down.

"I'll do it, Mike. And I'll do it for my regular fee. Anybody else, this could get expensive. But for you, I'll get it done."

"Thanks, Augie. There's one other thing."

"What's that, Mike?"

"This guy, Julian LaFete, has screwed a lot of people. He's shady. No, he's worse than shady, and he's probably desperate which could make him dangerous. You don't owe me any favors."

"Like I said, Mike, I'll get it done."

So, Mike explained the plan. He'd hit the Harris County district court house the next morning at eight o'clock sharp. Not a minute later. He'd get the TRO issued, which was intended to keep LaFete from doing anything with that car (sell it, drive it, *move* it from wherever the hell it was) and return it, within twenty-four hours, to Mike Buck's client, a lady CEO in the tech world. My job was to find Julian Lafete and serve him the TRO.

"Augie, I need you at the court house by eight, earlier if you can. My paralegal's got a pair of addresses for you; one's his business but I'm pretty sure it's a front to make him look legit. The other's an alternate address. It could be his residence. Augie, I can't emphasize how important this is. He's on the brink of bankruptcy and we think he'll dump the car and play dumb about its whereabouts. This guy is extremely sneaky and he's basically a crook. Augie, if you take this, nothing can interfere with it. I need top priority from you."

I assured Mike that he'd get August Spivey's full attention. I had a couple of other clients but their timelines were longer than Mike's. He put his paralegal, Dina Toomey, on the phone. She gave me the two addresses and a general description of Julian LaFete: mid-forties, brown hair, sideburns, six-feet-tall, a bit less than two hundred pounds.

"He's a weight-lifter, Augie. You can throw in martial arts. The black-belt variety. Did Mike mention that?"

"Not in that detail. He said he could be dangerous. Thanks, Dina. I'll take you out to lunch sometime."

It was four o'clock in the afternoon and I pushed

back from my desk. I put my invoices in their envelopes, addressed them, and thumbed a postage stamp into each of three corners. The mailbox was at the end of the street. Sandy was at her daughter's house overnight and our dog, Luther, was napping on the rug near my easy chair. I took a short walk to the mailbox, tossed the letters in, then headed home. I fed Luther a can of dog food, watered-up his drinking bowl, then threw a salad together for myself that I coupled with a slice of pepper jack cheese toast which I washed down with a glass of pomegranate juice my doctor suggested for a healthy prostate. After dinner, I settled into a Louis L'Amour novel which was interrupted by Luther needing to visit the back yard. I hit the hay at nine, Luther at the foot of the bed. I tried to sleep, but with the next day on my mind, may as well have been running a marathon.

I got up the next morning at four. I might've gotten an hour of real sleep, by that I mean the deep variety, the kind a human being needs if he's to walk and talk and function minimally among the living. If I was God, I'd make sure everybody got a good night's sleep. And not once in a while, but *every* night. I don't think that's asking for much. If mankind slept better, the world would be a better place.

I gulped down a glass of cold skim milk, fed Luther and put him in the back yard, and then headed out the door at seven o'clock. I figured the drive, in traffic, to the courthouse at thirty minutes. I didn't want to chance running late, especially for Mike Buck. Traffic was moderate, and I pulled into a parking space at the courthouse at seven thirty, give or take. I waited there, trying to grab a power nap, until eight o'clock when the courthouse opened. I went through security, and then into the district clerk's office where I waited for Mike, or, if not him, the issuance of the TRO which would come through the district clerk's administrative staff. I had my cell phone ready. By 8:30, I hadn't seen or heard from Mike Buck. I called his office.

"Dina, where's Mike?"

"He's still in court."

"He said this was urgent."

"It is."

"So, what gives?"

"He can't get the TRO issued."

"Why not?"

"He got there early. He's normally the first attorney on the docket. Not today. There were four other attorneys there ahead of him, all seeking TROs. Doesn't it just figure?"

"What should I do?"

"He thinks he'll have the TRO by noon."

"Should I wait?"

"There's no point in that. Go start your day, but check in regularly. Is this your cell number?"

"It is," I confirmed.

I delivered an easy paper in the area, so the morning wasn't completely lost. Then I drove home. I had my phone handy in case Mike got his TRO sooner than expected. With my personality, that being the anxious type, and with no sleep, I felt whipped already. And instead of feeding myself positive thoughts, I worried about how I'd deal with LaFete if he was as dangerous as I was led to believe. Should I posture legally when I served him? Should I talk tough to him? Should I be polite? Should I be prepared to drop the paper at his feet if he didn't accept service? When I left the scene, would I need to make sure I didn't turn my back on him? What if he pulled a gun on me or tried to jump me? LaFete was probably a car guy of some sort. I had a feeling about that. Call it intuition. All the car guys

I've known have been tough. I'm not talking about car salesmen. Our dad was a car *salesman,* but not a car *guy.* He didn't get his hands greasy, he didn't work with engines. He didn't talk about the Hemi or get excited about the Indy 500.

I entered our house by ten in the morning. Sandy had been home, eaten a quick breakfast, and let Luther back in. She'd also walked him. She'd left again, this time to take her mother to the doctor. All of that was in a writing pad she keeps on the kitchen counter.

I killed an hour or so at my desk trying to organize the notes from previous jobs but my mind wouldn't stay still. I sat down in my easy chair and stroked Luther for several minutes. Wouldn't you know, I got sleepy and could've taken a nap, but there was no rest for the weary coming my way. I had to get back to the courthouse, but I wasn't taking any chances on a wasted trip.

"Dina, it's Augie. What's the status?"

"Nothing yet."

"What the hell's going on?"

"One of the other attorney's TROs is being contested. It's setting everything back. Can you hang loose?"

"Yeah, I guess I'll have to."

I tried rubbing on Luther again but it didn't work. Nap time was over. I must've startled my amygdala. Rather than sitting at home on high-alert, I went back to the courthouse and took care of minor business on my cell phone. I did a lot of walking around that building. I don't do well twiddling my fingers, waiting on things to happen.

At 4:30, I took Dina's call.

"They're ready, Augie. God, I'm sorry about this."

I walked directly into the district clerk's office. There were four women who ran the desk: two white ladies, a black lady and a Hispanic lady. I know them all by name. Typically, they're very helpful, genuine pearls in the sea of public service. I'm also always sweet as warm honey to them. I have found that a little politeness usually goes a long way.

"I've got to have that TRO today," I pleaded.

Genie, one of the white ladies, looked as tired as I felt. We were both having a rough day.

"Augie, we're up to our ears. I don't know what's going on."

"Genie, if I don't get that TRO served this afternoon, a very bad man could slip out of a tight legal predicament. Would you want that?"

I felt lousy, framing the problem that way. Genie and the other three ladies were always there for me when I needed help. But what could I do? August Spivey was in a pinch. I received the TRO at one minute until five. I'd have hugged Genie like she was one of my sisters if we'd have been outside. I giddy-upped out to my Toyota pickup and drove.

I headed north on IH 45 toward Conroe. It was five o'clock and I figured to be knee-deep in rush-hour traffic, but I caught a break and was at the tip of the traffic sword. I rolled along at seventy mph, five miles over the speed limit, watching out for John Law. I didn't need a ticket.

I traveled IH 45 for eleven miles. I took the off-ramp to the right and took another right onto Sandy Hill Road. There was nothing sandy about it. It was pock-marked with one hole after another on a stretch of asphalt I'm sure the county had forgotten. Every time my pickup bounced I thought about my next expensive repair. Sandy gets on me from time to time about the cleanliness of my Toyota. I don't take it to the car wash regularly, and my back seat is covered in maps and files. My vehicle is my office away from home. But I've always treated my vehicles with the superior care that health nuts treat their internal organs: I change the oil every two months, I buy new tires every three years, I flush the radiator every year, and I burn nothing but premium gas. My ride needs to start when the key gets turned, no coughing, no sputtering. My life could depend on it.

I drove four miles and took another right. Traffic was slow. I chewed on my lip, a habit I can't shake. But I didn't feel tired. My adrenaline was running like a river. As a rule, the more anxious I get, the less I notice exhaustion.

Trove, Inc. was addressed at 3901 Warehouse Drive. I pulled into the fenced (ten feet high, more or less) parking lot of an industrial strip comprised of twelve warehouse spaces. The complex was in the boonies: weedy fields bordered by a drainage slough, a ratty old barn off in the distance. Each warehouse unit had a loading dock and a metal garage door. From what I could tell, most of the spaces were occupied with labor-related businesses: a paint company, a motorcycle repair place, a car upholstery shop. You get the picture.

At the end of the strip was *Trove, Inc.* Nobody was around. Every business out there, *Trove Inc.* included, looked closed for the day. I parked at the base of a short, concrete stairway, my truck pointed back toward the street. My knee was giving me trouble, and if I had to leave fast, I didn't want to jump the six feet from the loading dock down to the asphalt below. The sun had dropped beneath a fence-line of trees off to the west. It was me, and me alone, on a loading dock in the middle of nowhere.

It's rare, but you can be lucky in this business. I've had guys bump into me as I've turned a corner. But in the world of civil process, where putting the lawsuit directly into a guy's hands is considered sirloin steak, you don't count on good fortune.

I looked into the window of *Trove, Inc.* hoping I'd see La Fete along with the corvette. I could get a picture of the car and serve him at the same time. But it wasn't in the cards. By now, shade had captured the entire warehouse strip, leaving me a wisp of light to work with. Other than a desk with a telephone in its corner, the space was empty: no car, no people, no apparent active business.

I went back down the steps to my car where I called Mike Buck's office.

"Nobody's here, Dina."

"You're there?"

"Yeah, right outside the address you gave me. I wanted a shot of the car if nothing else. I have a feeling Mike's client won't be seeing her corvette again."

"Do you think you can serve the TRO on him?"

"If I can find him. What was the other address you gave me for him?"

Dina read me the number of a P.O. box.

"I can't do much tonight. It's getting dark and the yard lights have gone on. And I don't need to explain myself to a security cop. Tell you what, I'll follow up on that post office box tomorrow and see where that takes me. This place, I'm pretty sure, is a dead-end."

"Anything you want me to tell Mike?"

"Tell him I don't like disappointing people, especially him, so I'm not giving up."

I jumped in my car and made a loop around the warehouse complex. The backside was more of the fenced asphalt and a gate that led to a dusty, caliche road which appeared, in the dark, to meander through a cluster of trees beyond which I couldn't see. I jotted a series of quick notes on a pad I keep in my console, then got out of there.

I had an especially hard opinion of myself as I

drove home. Mike Buck knew I was good at my job, probably better than most. But in my view of things, you either come through, or you disappoint people. When I was a kid, I played baseball. I wasn't bad. But by the time I was fifteen, I was burned out. I felt the pressure of playing great and winning all the time. So, I quit the game. It wasn't fun anymore. Other than a game of catch, I didn't go near a diamond. Then, ten years later, I played in a summer league. My game wasn't sharp, but it caught the attention of a junior-college coach from Galveston Island. He offered me a scholarship which I took him up on. But after a year, I hung it up for good. That amygdala thing.

When I got home, Sandy was ready for bed. I hadn't seen her in two days. She and Luther went into the bedroom while I opened up Louis L'amour. It didn't help much, but I slept for a couple of hours, maybe three.

The next morning, I was back at it again. I drove out to the warehouse space where I sat and parked, waiting for any activity out of *Trove, Inc.* Unlike the night before, a few of the businesses were open. People were moving around. Several pickups came and went. Nothing was going on with *Trove, Inc.*

It was ten when I hit a nearby post office. I'd called Dina and had her look up the nearest postal station. It was fifteen minutes away. I grumbled to myself the whole way there. I had the P.O. box number and an idea.

The post office looked old on the outside, but newly renovated on the inside. There was a long, thin table that allowed customers a surface upon which to write. Three postal workers manned a counter. I stood in line, waiting my turn. When I reached the counter, I gave the clerk, a skinny white-kid, a piece of paper.

"What's this?"

"It's a request for a street address."

"I can't do that."

"Sure you can, it's *your* form."

"I've never seen this before."

"Take a good look at the top. It references the Texas Rules of Civil Procedure. You see that?"

"Yeah."

"Then look at what's written: the parties to a law suit, the cause number, and the TRO."

He sighed deeply.

"I need to talk to my manager," he said.

"I'm OK by that," I answered. "I'm not leaving without it."

I looked at the line forming behind me. The other two clerks had picked up the slack, but I sensed I was becoming unpopular with the mailing crowd. It wasn't the first time I'd had to explain an address request to a postal clerk. From my experience, at least nine of ten clerks don't know the form. I waited patiently. It was clear the clerk had been up late, probably partying. His eyes were bloodshot, the pupils unfocused, his mind running on empty. I recognized the look. I'd seen it in many a mirror.

When I was a kid, drugs swept through southwest Houston like the flu. Some guys caught it, some didn't. If I could give the kid any advice it would be to keep his body clean, and his mind clear. But like most young guys, he'd probably have to learn the hard way.

"You were right," he said. He returned with my written request and the residential street address penciled in a space opposite the P.O. box number. I grabbed the paper and took off. Several customers gave me the stink-eye for holding things up. It didn't faze me. I've done plenty of waiting on people like them.

In the car, I made a phone call to Dina.

"I got the street address," I confirmed.

"Mike knows you're going the distance, Augie. He really appreciates it."

"Dina, are you by your computer?"

"It's my home away from home."

"Can you do one of those satellite-searches?"

"Sure."

I gave her *2111 Blue Mountain Drive.*

"Where is it?" I asked.

Things went silent for a minute or two while she looked.

"It's in a subdivision that sits…. I'll be damned."

"Directly behind the warehouse strip?"

"Yeah, how'd you figure that?"

"A good guess," I said.

"Dina, can you see the entire warehouse strip as well as the subdivision?"

"Yeah."

"Look on the backside of the warehouse strip. Is there a dirt road that leads from it?"

"Yeah."

"You're sure?"

"Yeah."

"Where does the road go?"

"I'd say it meanders for a quarter mile then joins a concrete street smack-dab in the middle of Julian Lafete's subdivision."

"Dina, stay nearby. I'll call you in a bit."

I made a beeline through mid-morning traffic back to *Trove, Inc.* A light had flickered in my simple mind. If La Fete had been in his office when I pulled up yesterday, all he had to do was sneak out his back door, get in his car, and drive down that dirt road to his subdivision. He came and went, unnoticed, through the back. I'm no genius, but I felt my brain cells high-five each other.

I pulled into *Trove, Inc.* and gave it one more try. Like both of my earlier attempts, the office was empty. I jumped into my vehicle and drove to the rear of the building. The gate that connected to the dirt road was wide open. A dumpster sat just inside the fence.

I turned slowly from the asphalt parking lot on to the dirt. It was eight feet wide, a mix of baked clay, dust, and tire ruts. In a Houston rain, you'd be on your phone to the nearest towing company.

I bounced along at less than ten miles an hour. To my right was a tree-line of hackberry trees, to my left, acres of high weeds. It was typical Houston terrain: windy, coastal plain interrupted by an occasional barbed-wire fence.

The road terminated at a concrete apron. A large, wooden horse, long enough to separate the dirt road from the subdivision, had been pulled to the side.

"Dina, you still in front of your computer?"

"I am."

I tucked my phone between my left shoulder and the ear that goes along with it.

"Dina, take me to La Fete's house. I'm where the dirt road meets the concrete."

"OK, Augie. Do you see an intersection directly ahead?"

"I do."

"That's *Blue Ridge Drive*," Dina directed.

I drove several hundred feet to a stop sign well within the subdivision.

"What now?"

"Take a right," she instructed. "There's another intersection two blocks up."

I drove the distance.

"I'm there," I answered.

"Now left."

"OK," I said.

"You should be at *Blue Mountain Drive*."

I saw the street sign that confirmed my location. I thanked Dina and crawled along, my mouth dry, my heart racing. I practiced some positive self-talk, but it didn't help. My amygdala was cranking up the volume.

Blue Mountain Drive was standard middle-class. Not the kind of neighborhood I expected a to find a bad-guy in. The house was average size, brick, with a two-car garage, and a pair of well-kept flower beds. The Saint Augustine lawn was a rich green, the driveway and the cement walk leading up to the porch were trimmed neatly. My pre-conception of La Fete was way off. I'd probably watched too many crooks on cop-TV who fronted their crime business behind restaurants and topless bars. *Trove, Inc.* was nothing like that on the surface, but it *did* have all the features of a cover: legitimate looking on the outside, a corporate name, a pretty sign in an industrial park with nothing real behind it.

I parked my pickup in the *go* position along the curb in front of LaFete's house. It was eleven am. I filled out the TRO as much as possible to minimize my time at the front door. I walked along the driveway, not wanting to come up the middle of the yard. There was a newspaper on the driveway, telling me that LaFete was a late-morning guy. I noticed, through a windowpane in the garage door, a large vehicle, probably an *SUV,* but not the corvette.

I walked along the porch to the front door where I took a deep breath. I'd been in similar situations hundreds of times but I could never shake the anxiety. I know of three private eyes in the last several years who have died delivering civil process: one had his brain punctured by a nail embedded in a two-by-four, one had been shot, the third one got eaten by a pair of watch-dogs. I never know what's on the other side of a door.

I knocked loudly and waited. A light knock won't do. The guy behind the door has to know somebody's come a calling. Otherwise, he or his lawyer can say he didn't know he was being served if you resort to substitute service. Like any profession, the delivery of civil process has important steps. I follow those steps to the letter.

I heard someone approach the door. It opened. A pleasant rush of something cooking, probably bacon, hit me. Julian LaFete, wearing baggy gym shorts and a white T-shirt surrounded by a terrycloth robe, stood before me. He needed his morning shave. I figured he'd be on the angry side, but he was calm, make that stoic. Sociopath? Martial arts training? Who knew?

"I'm August Spivey. Sorry to bother, but I have a citation for you."

He took the paper from my hand.

"But, what is it?" he asked.

Most people don't like to be sued. But TROs carry an extra bite. You give a guy a piece of paper that says he can't go near somebody, or that he has to quit doing something *right now,* he tends to go from zero to sixty in four seconds.

"I'm not a lawyer so I can't speculate on that. But if you read the document, it will tell you what you need to know."

I turned and walked slowly, not once looking back, to my truck. I pulled away, drove a mile, then stopped in the parking lot of a convenience store where I made my notes. My hand was shaking.

I called Dina Toomey who put me on the phone to Mike Buck. I was his hero, but I knew that was only good until the next time he needed me. In that respect, Mike's no different from the others.

I drove home slowly, winding down from the adrenaline. Whatever was cooking in the LaFete kitchen made me hungry. I'd have a couple of eggs and sausage when I got home. I'd try to sleep, and maybe take Luther for a walk.

I thought about the man I just served. Scattered around his front yard were several pumpkins, all of them smiling, carved up for Halloween. That told me he probably had a wife and kids. Maybe he wasn't bad through and through. Maybe he had a soft bone or two. Anybody who takes care of his children can't be all bad.

20

THE "GO" POSITION

I wanted to serve Bud Lewis at his place of business. I *didn't* want to serve him at his home. But things don't always work out the way you plan.

I did some business with Jimmy Jack Darnell. Jimmy Jack is a big-time civil process server out of Dallas who I've been told serves over two thousand papers a month. Typically, I work directly with attorneys or their paralegals but in the case of somebody like Jimmy Jack, I'm a third party who he farms the paper out to.

There are people in my business who think Jimmy Jack is a dumb redneck. Maybe it's the name. He is anything but dumb. He runs a very tight ship. He is also tough as a cactus.

Jimmy Jack doesn't take phone calls. You don't call him; he calls *you*. And that is rare because everything is email with him. I check my emails three times a day: first thing in the morning, at noon, then around ten pm before I go to bed. I hate the electronic world. Computers are a major source of worry for me. But that's the way it is.

I never know when a Jimmy Jack paper will come my way. I'll open my email and there will be a request from Jimmy Jack to serve a paper. He'll give you the particulars, such as the party to be served, the address, etc., and if you accept, he mails you the papers along with your check up front. Jimmy Jack likes to get as much out of me as he can for one price. That's a problem for me because I like to bill when the job is over. I bill according to the number of attempts I have to make over and above my base fee. It's always possible that in addition to my base fee of $55, I might add on $10 per additional trip if I can't catch the party at the reported address. Very few papers get served on the first attempt. You got to be thick-skinned and persistent in this business. But Jimmy Jack sends me plenty of paper so I don't turn him down.

Like most people in the very-difficult world of lawsuit paper, and that includes lawyers, paralegals, and other process servers, Jimmy Jack Darnell is a pain in the ass. And so are the people you serve because, as a general rule, and I've been at this twenty-five years, no one likes being sued.

Which brings me back to Bud Lewis. Lewis owned a small cafe in Bunt, Texas, a dinky stop south and east of Houston. It's got a main street, a few storefronts, and a population of three hundred if you believe the sign that welcomes you. It's a dying town thanks to a Walmart that's twenty minutes away. I was familiar with Bunt thanks to several trips I'd made there for Jimmy Jack. I've always done good work for him, so I suppose he considers me one of his *"go to"* guys.

I took the address for the *Coffee Cup Cafe* and set off for Bunt bright and early on a cloudy day in March. I never know what's coming my way when I serve a paper. Sometimes the stuff I think will be hard turns out easy, other times you think a serve will be easy and it turns out crazy. I delivered a paper one time to a black man who I was told was not only big but mean as hell. The guy was every bit as big as advertised (6 feet 6 inches easy and creeping up on 300 muscular pounds) but he couldn't have been nicer or more polite when I handed him the paper.

I parked on Main Street, took the paper from my briefcase and went in. The *Coffee Cup Cafe* was what I expected in a small town: a clean, but scuffed floor, ten small tables (card-table size with two chairs each) scattered around and a pair of booths on two of the four walls. There was a counter upon which sat a cash register at the left end, a swinging door that led to the kitchen, and a pass-through window on the other side of the counter that gave me a view of a large, sweaty white man in a cook's hat and apron flipping something with a spatula. An anglo waitress in a white skirt and blouse hung out behind the counter. The place smelled good. Something was cooking in grease. Bacon and eggs maybe. It made me hungry. I thought about having a meal before serving Bud Lewis but, like it is with all my work, wanted to get in and out fast. God would have done mankind a great favor by making greasy food good for you.

I looked around for Lewis. In Jimmy Jack's email he described Lewis as sixty years old, white, and chubby. There was a man sitting at one of the tables who was too thin and too young to be Lewis.

I walked directly to the counter where the waitress stood. Up close she looked about forty and, with a little imagination, not bad looking. Her hair was dark brown. She had high cheek bones and, except for a few wrinkles around her mouth, smooth skin. Her name tag said *Liz*. A guy could do worse.

"I'm looking for Bud Lewis," I said.

"Not here," she said. "And he isn't here much which is OK by us." She looked over her left shoulder at the cook who turned her way and winked.

"Where does he live," I asked. "I've got court papers to serve him."

"Don't know," she said. "Never been to his house and don't intend to. Johnny, you know where Bud lives?"

"I do not," said Johnny the cook.

I jumped in my pickup and headed homeward. I felt discouraged. Make that anxious. Make that discouraged and anxious *both*. I've missed serves on my first attempt plenty of times. And, like I said, I expect it. It was the part about them not wanting him around that made me figure Lewis for a tough serve. Something just told me that.

I got home and went right into my office. Sandy and I live in a nice place not far from Loop 610. We have three bedrooms. One is ours, one is a guest room, and one we converted into my office

My office is a mess. It holds a file cabinet, a desk, my computer and printer, and a table that runs the length of a wall. I keep telling myself to clean the table off. It holds stuff going three and four years back. Whenever I walk into my office I worry I'm turning into one of those guys who hoards everything.

I was hungry and the smell of the *Coffee Cup Cafe* was still on my mind. It was eleven o'clock. I made myself a plate of bacon and eggs that I chased down with hot black coffee. I had half a grapefruit, a sweet roll, and one more cup of the black coffee. I don't drink coffee after twelve noon. I read somewhere that caffeine can stay with you for up to fourteen hours. I sleep little enough as it is.

I sat down at my computer and sent Jimmy Jack an email that laid out my unsuccessful trip to the *Coffee Cup Cafe*. A minute or so later my cellphone rang.

"Jimmy," I said, "I think he's avoiding. He wasn't at the cafe, and his help says he's never around. I can't figure he runs a business that way."

I held my breath a little. Jimmy Jack has a short fuse. When people go off on me I tend to go off on them. That's no way to keep things good between people. My experience with a lawyer by the name of Neal Green has taught me that. I didn't need another Neal Green playing ping-pong with my guts. But Jimmy Jack was polite which had me thinking I caught him on a good day.

"Don't worry, Augie, we'll skip-trace him," he said.

By *skip-tracing* Jimmy Jack meant he had software that can find someone no matter where they live. It's expensive and only the big-leaguers like Jimmy Jack can afford it. I find people by checking tax records, old phone books, knocking on doors. The business is passing me by. I can't keep up with the young guys who have the technology and the savvy to compete in the modern private investigator world. But I'm still around.

"Ok, Augie," said Jimmy Jack. He came up with Lewis's home address in less than a minute. "He lives out county road 9190. You know the area?"

"Yeah," I answered. And I did. And it scared me.

The area that Lewis lived in was rough. Barbed-wire, run-down manufactured homes, pit bulls (some chained, some not), I served paper out there before and swore I wouldn't go back. But bill collectors and grocers make for great motivational folks.

I went on the internet and found Lewis's place. You see, once I have an address I'm back in the game. It's the damn locating part of the job that drives me nuts. I drove down 9190 slower than slow, no more than five miles an hour. The road had holes and ruts so deep it would meat-grind a vehicle. I was already regretting taking the paper.

I found Lewis's place. A wide gate was open leaving a straight shot from the county road up a gravel driveway to a small house that sat about one-hundred feet off the road.

I reached into my glovebox and pulled out a laminated card that identified me as a court-ordered process server for the State of Texas. The card was attached to a string loop that allows me to wear it around my neck. I wanted it highly visible. Like I said, I smelled trouble.

The house was a dump. It was more of a dirty little cabin than a house. The paint was chipped and pealing. The railing on the front porch looked rotten. Part of it had torn loose and had fallen to the lawn below. There was no skirting under the porch, which gave me a look at a mama cat and her nursing litter. A damp smell was coming from somewhere. The shingles were peeling back in places on the roof. I figured any type of rain would soak the place inside. There was an outdoor toilet about fifty feet from the side of the house. When the wind blew from the north I'm sure whoever lived there got a good sniff of shit with their meal. And this guy owned a cafe?

I purposely stopped my pickup about thirty feet or so from the front door. I wanted it made clear I was no threat and was highly respectful of the property. I pulled the keys from the ignition, rolled down my window on the driver side, and shook them. It's a habit of mine. If there's a dog nearby I want to know. No dog stirred.

I grabbed the lawsuit paper which sat freely on the passenger seat next to me. With my left hand, I opened the door latch and began getting out. Just as my left foot hit the gravel I heard tires breaking. I looked in the rear-view mirror as a van pulled up behind me only inches from my back bumper. I got out of the pickup slowly.

Before I knew it, the guy who fit Lewis's description was out of the van and within a foot of me. In his right hand, he held a gun. He pointed it directly above my belly button. I don't know what kind it was. I don't know a Glick from a Glock. I don't own a gun. I can't imagine carrying one. It was one of those handguns that you put a clip into. I held my hands up over my head.

"I'm here to serve a paper," I said.

He wore a T-shirt, blue jeans, and a ball cap. He

looked to be about sixty years old.

"I don't give a Goddamn why you're here."

He nudged me with the barrel of the gun.

"You could get shot and I wouldn't have a legal problem in the world, " he threatened.

I thought about dropping the paper at his feet which Texas law allows if the party won't accept it. But I thought he might shoot me. He looked ready to crack.

"Do you know what a purple stripe means?" he asked.

A word here about the purple stripe. It's a substitute for a *No Trespassing* sign. It's been the law in Texas since 1997; a crime of trespass in the Texas Penal Code. But the stripe has to be at least eight inches long, at least one-inch wide, and three to five feet off the ground. It has to be clearly visible.

"I know exactly what it means," I said.

"And you didn't see it?" he asked.

"No, I didn't," I answered.

"Well, I think you did," he said.

"Like I said, I'm here to deliver paper."

"And like *I* said, I don't give a Goddamn why you're here. Now get the hell off my property."

I nodded. He got into his van and backed it away from my bumper. I backed out from his driveway onto the county road. Before I left I spotted the purple stripe on the bottom rung of the open gate. It was horizontal and somewhat hidden by weeds. It wasn't clearly visible. But he wouldn't get a purple-stripe lesson from me. I was tempted to speed away. My adrenaline was flowing like a river. I took it slow, remembering what the road could do to my truck.

Before I get angry I normally get scared. The scared part was behind me. By now I was pissed off. My mother hated bullies. She taught me two things about them: Don't become one and if one hits you don't leave until you've hit him back. I let myself get bullied on the receiving end of a gun. The next time I saw Lewis would be in a public place. If he pulled shit with me I'd break him open like a Luling watermelon.

I got home and went straight for my office. Sandy was out walking our dog, Luther. She walks him twice a day; late morning and late afternoon. It's good for her. It's good for Luther. It's good for me.

I emailed Jimmy Jack immediately, telling him what happened with Lewis. His phone call came back fast.

"OK, Augie," he said, "we'll go substitute-service on him. Send me your facts. I'll build the affidavit and get it to a local judge. What do you want in the order?"

I was ready with my answer. I had a slow drive down a bad road to think about it.

"Make sure I can serve anyone over the age of eighteen who works at his café," I said.

The process for getting an *Order for Substitute Service* can take a while. After several diligent attempts at serving a guy it becomes clear he's dodging you, a motion is drawn up. It and a sworn-affidavit are presented to a judge who, if he or she agrees, issues a court-order that allows you to serve someone over the age of eighteen, other than the original party, at the location specified in the order. My brother Jack, a lawyer, tells me that before you can sue a guy you have to give him notice of the suit for due process. I'm the notice guy. I'm part of the due process thing.

Three weeks went by. I stayed busy with a couple of papers from Neal Green that were surprisingly easy serves. Neal and I got along fairly well. I also got a job from a suspicious husband who thought his wife was playing naughty on him. I followed his wife, a woman in her thirties, to a crummy little motel on the East side. Sure enough, she met a young kid, college-age at most. I caught them on film going into the motel. They came out three hours later. I got that on film too. What went on inside, I don't know. I'd let her and my client work that out.

I got the order emailed to me by Jimmy Jack. I went over it like a hawk. I'm not a bad reader. I wanted it clear about who I could serve. I wanted this over and I wanted no complaining from Jimmy Jack who so far had been unusually nice.

The night before my drive to Bunt I didn't sleep. That didn't surprise me. My mind raced through one scenario after another, all of them ending with me confronting Bud Lewis in a bad way. I hoped he wouldn't be there in his cafe, and I hoped his indifferent waitress was behind that counter.

I pulled into Bunt at about nine. Main Street was mostly empty. The farmers in the area had already stopped by for their morning coffee and were back at coaxing a living out of Mother Nature.

I parked my Toyota in what I call the "go" position. I figured that strategy out on my second job as a private investigator twenty-five years ago. I make sure my vehicle is pointed in the direction of my escape, and I leave the door on the driver's side resting like it looks closed, but it's not latched. If trouble comes, I'm in the car and gone in a flash. The "go" position has saved my neck more than once.

I walked into the *Coffee Cup Cafe* expecting Bud Lewis to come flying at me but the place was quiet. No one was there. A clicking noise came from above. I looked up. The ceiling fan was turning slowly. That bacon and egg smell was in the air but this time I didn't get hungry. The outhouse upwind from Lewis's cabin came to mind.

I walked to the counter. My latest, favorite waitress was missing. Through the window I saw the cook. I recalled his name.

"Johnny," I said.

He looked up from his stove.

"Yeah," he answered.

"We need to talk," I said.

He came out through the swinging doors and stood the other side of the counter next to the register.

"Is Bud Lewis here?" I asked.

"No," said Johnny. "

"And he isn't here much which is OK by you," I filled in.

The smart-ass in me invites trouble from time to time but by now I figured Johnny and Liz to be part of Bud Lewis avoiding me.

"Here," I said. He took the lawsuit paper from me. "This is a lawsuit that involves Bud Lewis. He doesn't get this, it's on you. Are we clear Johnny?"

He nodded. I left the *Coffee Cup Cafe* looking over my shoulder. I did the same out on Main Street, Bunt, Texas. As I drove I felt the relief I always do when a tough job is done. I'd go home, email Jimmy Jack Darnell about my success. I'd also let him know I was done serving papers on county road 9190. It wasn't worth the danger.

Bud Lewis was in my head. I've served a lot of people. Some are angry, some don't give a hoot. Lewis looked worried. I couldn't recall that look before on any of the people I'd come across in my work. Like me being there with a lawsuit was just another heavy rock on his back. Like life was wearing him down so bad there was no getting up. Another time, another place, a different circumstance, he and I could've sat down and had a friendly visit.

21

TWENTY-NINE BARS

My brother, Jack does business in the following manner: if the legal advice he gives you turns out to be wrong, he promises to have your back and stand on the carpet with you. But if he gives you advice that turns out to be correct, you better have taken him seriously because if you didn't, and things go bad, he won't pull you out of the quicksand.

I've been in the private eye business for twenty-five years. For me, it's a mix of undercover work, surveillance, and civil process delivery. The undercover work, I like the best. It's safe, usually in a four-star hotel, and pays good. The surveillance work, I like the least. You sit and wait for hours at a time, normally in your car, parked in a subdivision, hoping that none of the neighbors gets the wrong idea about you. Civil process is dangerous. It's what keeps me up at night. Couple that with the strict time line that process serving involves, it's highly stressful, low-pay work. But it is regular, and covers my overhead.

Jack also preaches preparation. Every year we have a serious talk about my professionalism. It's a talk I don't look forward to. Jack reminds me that professionalism is more than the license I carry around in my wallet. It's also about *how* I carry *myself* in public. Once I'm out the door, the whole world is watching. I can let my hair down in the privacy of my home but nowhere else.

So, after twenty-five years in the business, wouldn't you know I got a call from the P.I. Board telling me I was looking at an audit?

"Jack, I've got everything I need."

"That's good," said Jack.

"But I'm missing one item."

"You said you had everything. What is it you're missing, Augie?"

"Let me tell you first what I *do* have."

"OK," Jack agreed.

I went on to list for Jack that I had my insurance certificate, my assumed-name certificate, my pocket-identification card, and my latest renewal certificate from the Board, all of it placed neatly and professionally in a manilla file I had labeled, "Augie's License."

"So, tell me what you *don't* have," insisted Jack.

And this is where things got uncomfortable because, even-though I knew that I was current on my continuing education, I couldn't find the certificate-of-proof which, as I looked back, had probably been thrown out in my latest office purge.

"Who administered the test?" asked Jack.

"PIAT," I said, and by that I meant the Private Investigator's Association of Texas of which I was a longtime, dues-paying member.

"What should I do, Jack?"

"Contact PIAT."

"But what if they don't have my record?"

"They will."

"But what if they don't?"

"Then your license will be suspended."

I knew enough to let it go there. We were on the phone, but I could hear steam coming out of Jack's ears.

"OK, Jack, I'll handle it."

"You do that, Augie."

I spent the rest of the day worrying. Work wasn't coming in, bills were due, and now this. There were two

Jacks competing for my attention: one named Spivey, the other named Daniels. I'd broken things off with that Daniels fellow a year or so ago, but I missed him like vegetation misses moisture. Jack Spivey could get in my head and drive me crazy. Jack Daniels could get in my head and make it go numb.

It was past five o'clock, too late to phone PIAT. I didn't eat much dinner which surprised Sandy. I normally have a good appetite. I thought about spending thirty minutes or so in the garage. I hadn't exercised in weeks, another thing Jack rides me about. When I'm disciplined, I workout in my garage gym. I ride an exercise bike, I do my sit-ups, I work hard on a heavy bag Jack bought me. But when I'm anxious or depressed, as I was then, I don't sleep, and when I don't sleep, I don't have the motivation to exercise. I was in a downward spiral.

I got up the next morning at four and I killed an hour at my desk getting nothing done. Sandy had enough of me prowling around the house, so she sent me out the door with Luther for his walk. That took another hour. When I got home, I showered and forced down a piece of buttered toast and a steaming cup of decaf coffee which I'd gotten into the good habit of drinking. I watched some morning TV while the clock went *tick-tick-tick*.

Finally, eight o'clock came. I called PIAT. If you don't get through early, it can be a long day. An older woman answered the phone. I explained, in short terms, my predicament. As I expected, she put me through to the extension of Connie Rogers, the head of continuing education. And, as I expected, I got her answering machine which directed me to leave the standard info: the time, my name, my number, and a brief message. She promised to get back to me as soon as possible. I kept my message short, but let her know, in desperate terms, that my audit

210

was scheduled for Tuesday (it was Friday as I made the call) and my license might be riding on obtaining copies of my continuing education results. I left her my cell number and hung up.

By noon I hadn't heard anything from Connie Rogers. There was a boxing match going on in my head and it was too early to call a winner. I sat down on our patio thinking about the countless times I'd figured my private eye game was over when a job would show up, things would break loose, and I'd make it through another month. It was hell going through times like this. I kept my fingers crossed. Luther was lying on the cement next to my chair. He can tell when things aren't right with me. He gave me a look he keeps just for me when I'm in the dumps. What would I do without Luther?

I got up from my lawn-chair, gave Luther a stroke on his head, and Sandy a kiss on the cheek as I left for my P.O. box. My box is located in a postal station four miles away. I check it three or four times a week. When the checks are rolling in, I'm happy. I can't think of anyone who doesn't like money.

I pulled into the postal station, found a parking space, and walked slowly into the building. I tried to keep focused on the problem in front of me. I couldn't shake my worry over the audit. My license was on the line and I had myself to blame. If one of my legs had been longer, I'd have kicked myself in the ass until it turned purple.

I produced my box key and opened the metal door. Except for a post card, the box was empty. I took the post card, gave it a brief once-over, and saw that it was an ad. Rather than toss it in the garbage can near the door, I stuffed it absent-mindedly into my breast pocket. I crawled into my Toyota and drove home. It was three in the afternoon and still no Connie Rogers.

I laid around the living room for an hour, alternating between boredom and worry. Come Monday morning, I'd call Connie Rogers and try to light a fire under her. A few minutes before 5:00, I looked at the post card. It was a general offer, from a law firm in Los Angeles, to private eyes in the Houston area. I had nothing to lose by making a phone call.

"You're familiar with theft of services?" The voice on the other end was young, polite, and middle-class white.

"I am," I answered.

"That type of piracy is not victimless," she said, "and the law firm for which I work has been hired to expose that type of piracy. Would you be interested? It pays rather well."

"Indeed, I would," I said.

She launched into the particulars: should I take the job, I would be expected to film a thirty-second clip of the Manny Paquiao-Jessie Vargas fight in progress on the bar TV. I would also be expected to capture, on camera, the bartender working that night. The following day, also required of me, was footage of the front of the bar and the satellite dish located somewhere on the premises. There would be an affidavit, executed by me, attesting to the facts surrounding the piracy. And, there was a catch. For every bar I found illegally pirating the fight, upon gathering satisfactory proof, I would be paid seven hundred dollars. However, for those bars not pirating the fight, there would be no minimum fee for my work. It was pure hit-or-miss.

I accepted the work. Within the hour, emailed to me was a list of the two hundred bars in Houston that had legally subscribed to the fight. My job was to find those bars which were not on the list and were illegally showing the fight. I also signed, electronically, an agreement that contained the terms of our deal, and my professional credentials, the whole time worried sick about the future of my license. I had twenty-four hours to formulate my game plan.

I pulled a map of Greater Houston and plotted, along IH 45, my route. With my list of approved bars as a guide, I would start in Conroe, Texas and drive south, stop at every dive I spotted, and finish near the Astrodome. I would simply stick my head in each bar, ask if they were televising the fight, and, if not, move on. I figured to spend no more than two or three minutes at any one stop unless I found an illegal broadcast. And, I had to move fast. Figuring three undercard fights, then the main event, along with interviews and commercials, the night would run no more than four hours. Any way I looked at it, the job was better than sitting at home waiting for things to happen. If I nailed just one renegade bar, I was looking at good money. Two bars, that would be a fourteen-hundred-dollar night. I didn't sleep worth a damn.

Saturday night couldn't come fast enough. Sandy and I bought groceries that morning, and from noon on I toyed with the idea of backing out. I was purposely targeting dives, the kind of marginal places that wouldn't pay for the subscription. But those were the rugged types of bars where a guy could get hurt. What if they caught me filming? I have a secret mini-camera installed in my key fob. I point and film, but that doesn't mean I can't be spotted. I could get bounced out of the bar, or even worse, take a beating in the parking lot. At five, I gave Sandy a peck on the cheek and stroked Luther one time for good luck. I promised Sandy I'd call her every thirty minutes with my location. I took off for Conroe.

I hit twenty-nine bars in four hours. Every one of the places I visited was near- empty. There was not one instance of pirating. If this had been March of 1970, the places I visited would've been lousy with people, all of them drunk, all of them screaming for their guy. But it wasn't 1970, this was no Ali-Frazier, and the big-boy heavyweights were a thing of the past. Think about it: Ali, Joe Frazier, George Foreman, Ken Norton, George Chuvalo, Oscar Bonavena, Larry Holmes, Ernie Shaver, The Spinks brothers, Jerry Quarry, Jimmy Young, Ron Lyle. And there were more!

The last bar I visited was the *Fly On The Wall*. It sat atop a tired-looking hamburger joint with a small neon sign. Access to the bar was up a narrow staircase that ran along the side of the hamburger place. I stuck my head inside the door. Like the other bars I'd visited, it was low-rent and dark with a few people scattered around, their heads down, cigarette butts piled high in ashtrays, the stink of stale beer in the air. Jack refers to such places as "therapy" bars.

The guy working the bar looked to be the owner. Don't ask me why, but I figured it that way. He had about ten years on me, a scraggly beard scribbled over a worn-out, pasty face.

"You showing the fight tonight?" I asked.

"This ain't no sports bar," he answered.

I went home, showered, and hit the hay. Monday morning, I got Connie Rogers on the phone who emailed me the continuing education certificates. On Tuesday, I came through my audit with flying colors. I had something good to tell Jack.

My first color TV was a Sony. Before that I watched the fights on Jack's portable black and white. I'd borrow it from him on the promise I'd have it back in a day or two. But more often than not, two days would turn into two weeks and I'd keep Jack's TV until he came knocking on my door.

I bought my color Sony for two hundred bucks. It meant a lot to me. I was bartending at the time and hadn't moved to Arizona where my private eye plan was hatched.

I had a buddy, Blacky Upjohn, I'd bartended with for several years. I assumed he was a pal, but that's the story of life, you live and you learn. I didn't know it at the time, but Blacky had a love affair going with meth. He hid it well. I'll give him that. I left him with my TV under the condition that he take care of it, and that in a couple of weeks I'd make a trip back to Houston from Arizona and pick it up. I never got that TV back.

22

AND I CALL MYSELF A PRIVATE EYE

I served paper on a guy who came to the front door in his pajamas. It was early, before he went to work. If a guy doesn't answer the door, because he wants to avoid me, I sit and wait on him until he breaks down and comes out of the house. I've sat down on people plenty of times, sometimes all day long. Unless they're rich, eventually they've got to go to work. I get between a guy and his paycheck, my success rate goes way up.

The fella asked me what the lawsuit was all about. I told him I was no lawyer but my guess was he needed one. And frankly, I don't read the lawsuit; I just deliver it. He yawned and took the paper nice and polite. Then he shut the door. No insults, no cussing, it was the kind of process delivery any private eye would be grateful for.

On my way home it started to rain. It came down hard—*scary hard*—in sheets. I couldn't see much beyond the front of my Ford Edge SUV. (My red Toyota pickup had finally died.) I walked in the door with my stomach scolding me. I skipped breakfast earlier that morning. I was in a hurry to take care of business so I'd gulped down a glass of ice cold milk and called it a meal.

I slept good the night before which sort of surprised me. I normally don't sleep well when I'm serving paper. I toss and turn worrying what I'll be up against or what I might mess up. Dropping paper is rarely easy. The man in his jammies was an exception to the rule. And if you get a reputation for being sloppy, no lawyer or paralegal will touch you.

Sandy was away at work so the dog and I had the morning to ourselves. I filled Luther's bowl with the best dog food money can buy. Sandy and I take good care of Luther. He's a shelter dog, a mix of pit bull and a labrador. You come in the house, he knows you, he'll slobber your clothes wet. He doesn't know you, you best have your Last Will and Testament in your back pocket.

I opened the ice box door wanting meat. Sandy and I hadn't gone shopping in a while so we were down to a jar of Peter Pan, a jar of Welch's grape-jelly, a bag of rye bread, and that milk that I drank for breakfast. I shut the refrigerator despite my mother reminding me from the grave how hungry people were in China.

Slippey's was ten minutes away. Earl Slippey, a former boxer, is the owner; hence the name. You like barbecue to die for, Slippey's is your place. I called and ordered a *to go* plate with a brisket sandwich smothered in hot sauce, a lump of mashed potatoes, and a side of pinto beans. A beer would've been nice but I went with the largest and coldest iced tea in Texas. I threw on a jacket that was once my old man's. I ran out to my car; it was still raining pitchforks. I figured my trip up and back at twenty minutes. I left Luther alone in the house. I kept my fingers crossed hoping the dog wouldn't take a pisser or, God forbid, the big smelly.

I drove a block or so to a four-way stop. I could go left or right to reach Slippey's. Left was shorter but it had construction that would only increase my worry over Luther. I went right. It added distance, but on most days the route was open all the way to Slippey's.

I drove a quarter of a mile to the road that led up to the restaurant. I took another right. On my left was the local middle-school fronted by a one-mile stretch of two-way blacktop. Rain was pounding away. Mother Nature was in a bad mood. Up ahead was a low-water crossing that ran over a swollen creek. Common sense had me turning around and saying grace over peanut butter and jelly back at the house. But my tummy was driving things and August Spivey is not a patient man.

I stopped short of the bridge. Creek water was spilling out of its banks, moving from right to left. At the top of a small hill the other side of the creek sat Slippey's. A layer of water ran over the bridge. I told myself it looked doable. I moved ahead. I figured to start slow then gun it over the bridge and up to the Slippey's parking lot. Most things I can say, '*no,*' to. I can't say, '*no,*' to Slippey's. Great barbecue will do that to a man. Next thing I knew, my SUV was floating.

People ask me what it was like staring into all that peril. I tell them I was worried about my car. If I don't drive, I don't make a living. My SUV turned a complete circle, soft, bouncy like a ride on an inner-tube at a family waterpark. The spin gave me a full view of my circumstance. I forgot the car issue when I saw what was coming.

A few hundred feet to my left the creek elbowed. I was familiar with the creek. I'd seen it plenty of times when the weather was dry. The channel, roughly sixty-feet wide by forty-feet deep, had become a giant blender of whitewater, trash, and brush. Between me and the channel was a group of three hackberry trees along a fence-line I recalled but couldn't see.

I wanted *out* of that SUV. I tried the door-latch on both the driver and passenger sides. Neither budged. I tried the electric windows. I got nowhere. I pulled my legs from under the wheel, tucked them up, then turned and kicked with everything I had at the driver, passenger, and front windows until I was out of breath. I was trapped in a car that was headed for the deepest part of the creek.

At no time in my work have I ever figured I was dead. I've been scared to the point that only my friend, Jack Daniels, could calm me down. Pit bulls have chased me, guns have been leveled at me. I took a stroll down a dark hall in the projects no white man should take. None of that had me thinking about the Grim Reaper.

The SUV hit the tree bank hard. It spun around and faced back toward the road I'd driven in on. I felt the tail end of the SUV drop. To my left were the hackberry trees, to my right a tangle of barbwire and heavy growth, most of it under water. A waterfall crashed onto the hood and windshield with the force of an open hydrant. I felt a cold surge of water on my feet, ankles, and thighs coming up fast from the floor board. *That's* when I thought I might die.

How bad do you want to live, Augie? A voice! I *heard* it. I wore myself out kicking at the windows. I kicked, I rested, I kicked. Nothing was working. Water had filled up the entire cabin but for a small bubble of air, about the size of a basketball, in the upper right-hand corner of the passenger seat. I scooted over, my chest and head the only parts of my body not underwater. I resigned myself. This was how I was going to end.

Who in his life hasn't wondered what his death would be like and what happens afterwards? I grew up a Catholic but I hadn't received the sacraments in years. I still believed in God but had long since given up on dogma and the mumbo jumbo that goes with it. My soul was smudged up with bad acts but none of them dark and mortal. And yet, with eternity closing in, I was calm; calm like I'd never been in my life. *Wicked* calm.

I considered how I would go. I could hold my breath until the bitter end, my burning lungs sucking in water. Or I could accept the water naturally, breathing it in best I could. I'd read somewhere that once your lungs filled with water, drowning wasn't so terrible. I wanted to meet the guy who came up with that.

The water was under my chin. I wondered how they would find me, *if* they found me. I took one last look in the sun-visor mirror. *Good bye, Augie,* I thought.

Then I saw it. In the mirror! Through the cabin filled with water I saw it. The hatch! Flapping in the water. I saw it. Yes, I saw it. *It couldn't be.*

I sucked in a gulp of air and forced myself past the headrests into the back seat. I did the same from the back seat onto the back deck of the SUV. I fought through my state of resignation and decided that Augie Spivey would not die in that car. It would not be my coffin!

The hatch was open. I was crazy for air. I pushed on the hatch and rolled out free and clear of the car. Things went from bad to worse. The current grabbed me. I felt for the hatch. It was there. I used it to pull myself up and out of the raging water. My head and shoulders free, I took in as much air as I could, panting and gagging on cold, brown water.

But it wasn't over. The creek still had me in the palm of its hand. I hung on desperately to the top of the hatch, the rush of water lifting me horizontally. I needed to make it to the trees. If I was going to live, I had to get to those trees.

With my left hand, I grabbed the luggage rack on top of the SUV. I followed with my right hand, pulling myself tightly to the left side of the car then working my way, inch by inch, along the luggage rack to a point above the windshield where the rack ended.

I lacked ten or more feet from my position on the car to the trees. The waterfall that was hammering the hood and the windshield hadn't let up. Rain was coming down sideways. I'd seen rain do that once in my sixty years. It was in Hurricane Carla. I was ten years old. She put most of the Gulf Freeway under water. People died. Fishing villages disappeared. I witnessed shingles fly off our neighbor's house like popcorn.

There was a vine dangling from the middle hackberry tree. I judged its distance from me at six feet. It looked thick enough to hold me if I could grab it. If I missed, I was in the channel. I took a deep breath and lunged for it, grabbed it with my left hand, then pulled myself hand over hand to the middle tree. That tree was the last thing between me and death and I hugged it that way.

What seemed like an hour went by. Who was keeping time? My watch and wallet were gone as were my windbreaker, shirt, and shoes leaving me bare-chested and barefoot. I kept my pants, but only because my belt held them up. The creek had almost undressed me.

The way I saw it, I was on the good end of two miracles: hitting those trees which kept me out of the channel, and the hatch which had opened when it did. Two more minutes, I was explaining my life to Jesus Christ.

I began thinking that I might get out of this alive. But I couldn't hold out for much longer. I was cold; my fingers were going numb. I thought about shimmying up the tree but I didn't have it in me. Running between my tree and the other two which flanked it was a large cable-like root. I leaned forward and draped myself over it allowing myself to rest. It had its price. Water crashed into me, sometimes sending me under. But I was able to gulp air between waves. Despite the fix I'd gotten into, I complimented myself on having no quit in me. Now it was all about riding things out.

Nothing changed for a while. I got busy on the Lord's Prayer. Anything God wanted, August Spivey was on board. A couple of things needed attention. I could be a better husband. I could drop some weight. Jack Daniels and I didn't need to see so much of each other. A little church now and then wouldn't kill me.

I was facing the road I'd driven in on and had a good view of the bridge. I figured about two hundred feet separated me from the road. A red pickup came along. It stopped short of the bridge, the driver no doubt deciding what to do next. He made the same mistake I did. The creek lifted his truck off its wheels just as it had my SUV. I wasn't the only guy on the planet nuts about Slippey's.

I like a good movie. When Sandy and I are looking for something to do we sneak out to the bargain matinee. There's a cinema close by where the two of us can see recent movies for less than ten bucks. I don't understand why people spend thirty bucks to catch a night-time movie.

Sandy goes for the romantic stuff. Boy meets girl. Boy loses girl. Boy gets girl back. Everybody goes home happy. I like the action movies. Surprised? Guys jumping off buildings, bombs going off. I don't need the blood and gore. Give me *Indiana Jones* or *Die Hard* or *Lethal Weapon* with that Gibson fella. I come out of a movie like that, I'm ready to tear the world a new asshole.

This should have been a movie but it wasn't. Oh no, this was real. A ton of red pickup was bobbing and spinning its way toward me. Its route looked almost identical to mine. The driver opened his window on the driver side, climbed out ass and arms first, then worked his way into the bed of the pickup. His agility was high-level. He pulled his cell phone from his shirt pocket and made a call. I was hoping 911 was on the other end.

I braced best I could along the tree root. I hugged it like it was family. I closed my eyes and tucked my head into my right arm. A strong wave splashed over me. I felt the truck hit. A shiver went through the trees. A force hit me under the water that almost blew me off my perch. I came up for air. The truck was on the front side of the tree bank where it had come in sideways.

The driver was black. I figured him for forty years old. He wore blue jeans, a plaid shirt, and a red down-vest. He had on a green ball cap which, far as I could tell, had no lettering. He had what I would describe as a military demeanor, that being calm and in charge. Or maybe he was an off-duty cop. He had authority written on him.

"Hey!" I yelled. "Hey!" I was surprised at how weak my voice was.

"Who's that?" he yelled.

He and I weren't six feet from each other but with my car on the other side of the trees and a curtain of weeds and thicket between us, he had no idea where my voice was coming from.

"Look down," I shouted.

He searched, then spotted me.

"Come on," he yelled.

"I can't," I said. "I'm whipped."

"Can you break through the brush?"

"I can't. I'll get rolled into the channel if I let go."

He reached over the side of the truck and began breaking twigs. In twenty minutes or so he carved out an opening, about the size of a manhole.

"Here," he yelled. "Grab my hands."

I did just that. Our hands met midway in the escape hole he had made. He pulled me through the bramble to his side of the trees. Sixty-year-old Augie Spivey had been born into a very dangerous world.

By now water was tumbling over the bed of the pickup. Another crush of water spilled over the side of the truck onto me.

"I can't do much more for you," he yelled. "It's all I can do to hold on."

And that was true. He was gripping the seam that ran along the back of the pickup's cabin.

"I can't make it," I said wearily.

"I'm sorry, buddy, I'm out of ideas."

He reached his left hand over the side of the truck, holding the seam with his right.

"This is it," he said. "You gotta do it."

How bad do you want to live, Augie? That voice again. It wasn't warm and cuddly. It wasn't angry, but it meant business. Live or die, my choice.

"OK!" I yelled.

The pickup was rising and falling as waves piled toward the channel. There was no bounce left in me. I was made out of lead. I timed my jump. At the height of the pickup's rise, I pulled with my arms hard as I could. I caught the side of the pickup on its way down with my right leg. The current splashing over the pickup bed tried to throw me back out. I felt a hand grab my belt, near my backside, that pulled me into the truck.

"Hold this," he yelled, "or you're right back in."

With his help, I stood up and grabbed the seam along the cab. The strength of the water hitting me at the knees told me we weren't out of this yet.

"I'm Lincoln," he yelled. "What's your name?"

"Augie," I shouted above it all. "Augie Spivey."

"Help's on the way," he yelled. "Hang in there."

We didn't talk much; no room for chit-chat. For the love of God, would the rain ever end? And I was cold.

Soaked to the skin, a driving rain, a November cool front, my teeth were chattering.

"Here," said Lincoln, "take this."

With his right hand, Lincoln slipped off his down-vest and passed it to me. With my free left hand, I worked the vest on over my bare torso as Lincoln helped.

"Thanks, man," I said, "but you didn't have to do that."

"Your lips are blue," he said.

"You think we'll get out of this?" I asked.

"Yeah," he said, "we'll make it."

We held our ground for another hour. My fingers were on fire from pinching the metal seam. I blocked out the pain best I could.

"Lincoln," I said, "I owe you my life."

"Don't think twice about it," he answered.

A pair of EMS units showed up out on the road. Lincoln and I both waved with a free hand, holding tight with the other. Screaming was unnecessary. The EMS responders saw us and several waved back.

I counted twelve uniformed responders: ten men, two women. The responders huddled for a few minutes, I figured to talk strategy. All but one woman put on life-jackets. A rope was fastened to the tail-end of one of the EMS units. Each responder tied himself to the other with fifteen to twenty feet of rope. Then they entered the water, one by one, single file, and came toward us. They arrived quickly.

"You go, Lincoln," I said.

"You go," said Lincoln.

The responder at the front of the human chain looked at me shivering.

"Here," he said.

He handed me a spare lifejacket that he had carried

with him. It was tough, but I got it on. A second life-jacket was with the responder who was next in line. He signaled the line of responders then tugged me into the water. It felt like ice. The line of responders, with me at its tail-end, began moving toward dry land.

"Don't forget Lincoln," I said.

I was in the EMS unit covered with blankets.

"We won't forget him," I heard a male responder answer.

I closed my eyes as the ambulance rumbled along. As far as I knew, Sandy had no idea what had happened. And Luther! Surely by now he crapped the floor. I was treated for hypothermia. I spent the night in the regional hospital. I tried to sleep but couldn't. Tired as I was, the day wouldn't go away. Finally, I asked for something to *make* me sleep. Valium put me under.

Sandy rushed over from work upon receiving a call from the hospital. My brother Jack chewed on me over the phone but it rolled off my back. I was right about Luther. He made a mess in the house.

I went fetal on the couch for a few days. I couldn't get enough warmth. You'd think after what I'd been through nothing would bother me again, but I started worrying about getting work; about keeping lawyers happy. My mother was a worrier. She went to bed late and got up early. I know. I watched her. I guess some people are born to worry.

Sandy handled the loss of my car. God bless her! I am not an easy guy to live with. The insurance adjuster grilled me over the phone. I gave him all the facts. And I made it clear the county hadn't put up barriers in front of the low-water crossing which led me to believe I could cross the bridge. We received a check for the full bluebook value of my Ford Edge which I turned into a used, late-model Ford Focus. It runs like a top.

A couple of days later, after I got back my strength, Sandy and I took a drive in her car. We pulled over on the side of the road near the low-water crossing with Slippey's in view. The creek had gone back into its banks; it was a small, slow stream. Mama Earth had dried out.

Sandy and I walked to the trees. With the creek back to normal, it was difficult to imagine the nightmare that had taken place. At first I couldn't find my SUV. Then I spotted its front bumper poking partially out of the mud. That was the only part of my car that wasn't buried. Lincoln's pickup was gone.

I talked Sandy into lunch at Slippey's on me. She drove over the low-water crossing slowly. I held my breath. I made it a point not to order the meal that got me into trouble. I considered it bad luck.

Sandy ordered a small rack of ribs and a scoop of potato salad. I had a quarter of barbecued chicken, some potato salad of my own, and a hot cob of corn dripping in butter. We each ordered unsweetened ice tea.

"You think at all about what happened back there?" she asked. It was her first time to visit the scene of my near-drowning.

"Yeah, I do," I said thoughtfully. "*When* that hatch opened. And something was talking to me. It wasn't just me in that car."

After lunch, I had Sandy run me by the hospital. I had unfinished business. I walked to the admitting desk where I recognized a nurse from the day I was brought in.

"I was in here the other day. I almost drowned."

She ran her eyes from left to right across the ER. The place was full of people. In her world, I was no superstar.

"Your name?" she asked.

"August Spivey," I answered.

I gave her the date and time of my stay at the hospital.

"There's nobody with the first name of Lincoln on that day," she said.

"Anybody at all come through that day who might've almost drowned? A black guy?"

"Nobody," she said.

Sandy and I drove home. We watched television. I couldn't tell you what was on.

"Did you think to get his plates?" she asked.

"No," I said and shook my head in disgust. "And I call myself a private eye."

AUTHOR'S BIO

Mike Keenan grew up in Houston, Texas where he attended elementary, high school, college and law school. He has spent all of his legal career in Austin, Texas and is now a retired attorney. Writing fiction has been one of his passions for over thirty years.

More Stories by Mike Keenan

The Georgellen Club

The Georgellen Club is a collection of short stories where the threads of the lives of its intersecting characters are tied together at a fictitious bar and restaurant in Galveston, Texas.

Excerpt from *The Owner,* a story from *The Georgellen Club*

I murdered a man. I didn't do it with my own hands. I paid someone to do it. I put it into motion. In the words of Tommy Aquinas, I was the "prime mover." And I have no regrets about my sin. The man who was murdered had it coming. He had done enough damage. If you are interested, here is my story.

I graduated from high school ambitionless. College was within reach, none of the elite institutions, but somewhere. However, I hated school. I saw no point in it,

229

which may have been a mistake on my part. I considered the army, but I knew that discipline and I were not compatible. My dad, a car salesman, made it clear to me I had to do something, if not school, or the military, then a job.

I wasted three years. I lived at home and tried a series of menial jobs. I looked in the newspaper. There were ads for delivery boys and phone solicitors. I tried a few. I worked at a car wash. I parked cars. I drove a cab. I sold cutlery (which lasted one week.) I refer to those years as my *period of doing nothing.*

One evening, my father away selling the cars that would fill my belly, I saw an ad on television. It was local variety, a thirty second clip that appealed to me. It seemed promising and, if nothing else, would get my parents off my back. I enrolled in the Night Owl School of Bartending.

Six weeks later I came out a bartender. It cost me three hundred dollars. (It cost my dad three hundred dollars.) I learned the art of mixology. Night Owl placed me into my first job as a bartender. I moved out of my parents' house and that's when I met the man I murdered.

I went to work at Woodley's, a bar restaurant in southwest Houston. It was a big bright place. The manager was easy to work for. It was in a strip center that's run down now. Woodley's is long gone. Last I looked the Woodley's space had been converted into a pawnshop and a convenience store.

I met Carter McCrae at Woodley's. We hit it off. He was a year older than me. We tended bar together. He showed me the ropes. We decided to room together. I'd been living in a one bedroom apartment a short drive from Woodley's. (I bought a used car from my dad.) Carter and I rented a house in Bellaire which is its own city engulfed by greater Houston.

Carter was a charming, good-looking guy who introduced me to the world of excess. He was a chick magnet. I was not. I watched with fascination as he picked up women and scored with them on a steady basis. It amazed me how he never seemed worried that a former conquest might drop in while he was engaged in his latest conjugation. But he had a basic understanding of people and upon reflection the bar material he was picking up was of the one night variety so there must have been a mutual understanding that come daylight both parties would go their separate ways.

I saw Carter McCrae change. The river of women who rolled through our rent house during the two years Carter and I lived together were all easy lookers. I didn't see any super models but they were all well above average. I was eating breakfast one morning (Woodley's was a night time gig) when a tall blond girl came out of Carter's room on her way out. She was nice. She shook hands with me. We actually chatted for a few minutes. Unlike the other women Carter seduced, this girl was a little on the plain side. (I'm being generous.) Just as we'd finished our conversation a brief look passed over her face. She excused herself and walked back to Carter's bedroom, fumbling with her purse as she pulled out a cluster of twenty dollar bills. And that is where it began for Carter.

It went on for about a year. The volume of women slowed down to what appeared to be a manageable clientele. Most were well dressed and, judging from their looks, undoubtedly lonely. I wish to be clear. Carter and I were not friends. Our relationship was strictly that of roommates. In defence of him, he was very responsible with money. He always came up with his half of the rent and bills on time. I never once had to remind him it was the first of the month. I didn't judge him at first. But I did not want an association with a male hooker. He eventually came to me and announced he was quitting Woodley's and moving out. He didn't tell me what he was going to do, but I gathered he was entering the big leagues of money for sex.

That was okay by me. I was making good money at Woodley's. I knew I could cover expenses by myself until I found another roommate. I was satisfied where I was. I'd been at Woodley's two years, my longest time on a job. I liked my boss, and I liked the foothold I'd gotten in life.

A week after he moved out, Carter called me. He had forgotten a picture of the Grand Canyon on a bookcase in his room. I knew the picture and knew how much Carter liked it. He pulled up in a brand new black Mercedes sedan. Carter had owned an old Ford pickup. The Mercedes caught me off guard. Before he could come in, I walked out onto the driveway. I held the picture. He rolled down the car window. On the passenger side was a woman at least twenty years older than Carter. He introduced her as Peggy Bosh. She, like the other recent women in Carter's life, was, to be frank, rather unattractive. To my surprise, Carter introduced her as his fiancé. She smiled. I reached across Carter and shook her hand. We spent a few minutes engaged in small talk. Carter thanked me for the picture. He suggested to Peggy Bosh that the Grand Canyon would be a good honeymoon spot. His fiancé invited me to the wedding when they set a date. I accepted but made no special note to myself about it. They drove off.

I kept an eye on the wedding announcements. I figured, surely, Peggy Bosh would see through Carter McCrae. But, no, lonely people are either very hard or very malleable. A month later I found their wedding announcement. Peggy Bosh looked happy. I felt sorry for her. I didn't know her and probably shouldn't have cared one way or another but I could see all that joy etched on her face coming to an end. Carter had no conscience about taking advantage of that lonely woman.

Find out how this story ends.

<u>Mike's books are available at Amazon.com</u>